TREADING WATER

Kate Pavelle

Published by Mugen Press
Pittsburgh, PA

Published by
Mugen Press
P.O. BOX 11061
Pittsburgh, PA 15237, USA
www.mugenpress.com

Treading Water

www.mugenpress.com
ISBN:9781942920007
Printed in the United States of America
First Edition
July 30, 2015

Swordfall

"... a thrilling adventure, full of excitement, hot sex, menace and ultimately a love between two men that won't be stopped short of death."
-    USA Today

Landfall

"This is a great ending to the series and another book that demonstrates Ms Pavelle's broad knowledge of science and martial arts as well as her vivid imagination."

- Becky Condit

Relativistic Phenomena

"Relativistic Phenomena is a sweet novella, and the tentative relationship between Tony and Ken is quite endearing."
-    Scuttlebutt Reviews

On the Run (a Cancelled Czech Files book)

"... a journey on the run from the secret police as they bravely immigrated to America... a book to read with your entire family."
-    USA Today

More by Kate Pavelle:

With Mugen Press (www.mugenpress.com)

Relativistic Phenomena
Kickass Anthology
On the Run (Cancelled Czech Files book)

Coming soon:

Lucky Starflowers (Steel City Stories)
Waterkin (urban fantasy YA)

With Dreamspinner Press (www.dreamspinnerpress.com)

Wild Horses (Steel City Stories)
Zipper Fall (Steel City Stories)
Broken Gait (Steel City Stories)
Breakfall (Book 1 of Fall trilogy)
Swordfall (Book 2 of fall trilogy)
Landfall (Book 3 of the Fall Trilogy

Coming soon:

Sire (Steel City Stories)

TO SUZANNA,

our fairy godmother of bikes and paddleboards,
who holds the unshakable belief that this fat, slow triathlete
can become a leaner, faster one!

SHAMELESS PLUG:

Our family, as well as the characters on these pages, get their bikes at
www.roadbikeoutlet.com

CHAPTER 1

THE MAN was in the pool again, struggling in the lap lane by the wall. His arms were fighting the water as though he was the blustery, early February wind. Just like the wind outside. The surface of the swim lane frothed under his assault, beaten as though it was a mortal enemy while the swimmer kicked to move ahead while struggling for breath.

Sebastian refocused on his personal trainer, trying his best to engage in his regimen. His time was, after all, limited. Blond hair slicked under his white AquaGlobe swim cap, gray eyes concealed by light-reflective swim goggles, he lifted his head out of the water and beckoned Yolanda down to his level.

"Perhaps you should give him some pointers," he said in a low voice. "I can't do my best work with all that splashing going on!"

"You're paying me, yet you'd have him trained on your own time?" Yolanda's catlike eyes crinkled in barely concealed mirth.

Anyone else would have grimaced. Sebastian Gillen, however, gave her a wry grin. "Think of it as an investment into my inner peace! I figured he'd be gone by now. All the other New Year's Resolution exercisers have already quit."

Lunch workouts used to be so quiet.

"Sure thing, Seb. How about you work on your cadence while I talk to him? Gimme five hundred meters, bilateral breathing, five strokes per breath."

He nodded and kicked off.

SEBASTIAN Gillen was a swimmer. He was also many other things besides, but swimming had been his passion since he fell into a pond as a child and discovered the sensuous feel of water against his body. He used to swim on school teams. His father had employed private coaches to advance his progress. Now, as an adult, he continued the soothing, meditative practice of striving for perfection with every breath, with every stroke. Yolanda Swan was irritating at times, but the instruction she provided was worth every penny. A former Olympic team swimmer, she delivered exactly what Sebastian needed—along with a heaping side of criticism that rankled spiced by fresh, merciless teasing.

Sebastian's own dream of a competitive, world-class swimming career died with his enrollment in a top MBA program several years ago. Now he was the Vice President and heir-apparent of the family business he was expected to run someday, and his days were spent analyzing ice cream market statistics, deciding upon new marketing strategies, and negotiating with vendors who carried Gillen Frozen Desserts.

He didn't like sweets.

He was lactose-intolerant.

He was a health-food freak.

Schlepping ice cream for living wasn't his idea of a lifelong vocation. The company made the money that put him through school and kept him comfortable. That, and a strong family tradition, made for a current too strong to fight. Despite his best efforts, he soon found himself floating downstream as he worked for the family, parents and uncles and cousins. They held stock and wanted to be paid quarterly dividends, along with dispensing opinions and their so-called helpful remarks, but seldom lending a hand.

Swimming was Sebastian's only escape.

JESSE WAS doing great. The office park had a gym, and the gym had a pool. He had started training on January 1st, along with the rest of the company employees.

At first he'd absolutely hated it. He didn't like being told what to do, and he especially resented being coerced. The choice, however, had been clear: participate in a company-sponsored triathlon, or be fired. A medical excuse would've made him unfit for a job at the security company, thus violating his employment agreement.

Jesse was stuck.

After the usual grumbling and back-talk, his coworkers had adjusted along with him and trained after work. Swimming, running and cycling hadn't sounded hard at first. Jesse, however, hadn't even known how to swim. Unless he wanted to drown in the river during his first ever triathlon, though, he would have to learn, and quickly

A TRIATHLON was a test of endurance, and when Jesse had been growing up on the reservation, he and his friends used "warrior games" to burn off their infinite, youthful energy. Grandpas and uncles had cheered them on back then and Jesse still remembered that ancient, mysterious feeling of tapping into the spirits of his ancestors to boost his strength, his courage, his endurance.

As he flailed in the pool and tried to access a source of strength he hadn't thought of in over fifteen years, an uncomfortable thought flitted through his mind.

Suppose he had lost it.

Suppose he just couldn't do it anymore.

Suppose it's been too long and he was now cut off.

Jesse's mother was half-Crow, and that made Jesse Crow, too, he reminded himself as he recalled his proud heritage and the wild days of his youth. He reached the end of the pool and hung off the edge for a while, catching his breath, thinking of that young boy who used to run the hills and climb the tallest trees.

That young warrior was still in there somewhere.

The boys he'd grown up with would have been thrilled at the opportunity to show that they were stronger, faster, and could last longer than their friends. That, however, had been thousands of miles west of here and many servings of junk food ago.

The sixty pounds he had gained while working a sedentary

computer job had piled on as he embraced his career and the East Coast sedentary lifestyle. His work was his life. Jesse hadn't done much else since he had dumped Renata well over a year ago. But not all was lost - the pounds that had weighed him down during his attempt at running now, ironically, helped him stay afloat in the water.

He splashed along for two hundred meters. That was eight times across the twenty-five-meter length of the pool, but it felt like much longer. Two months ago, he'd have been sitting at his computer, playing Warcraft during lunch and sitting by the computer some more, doing network maintenance for his boss Easton, had it not been for Easton's maniacal zeal. The 11th Hour Security Company owner believed all of his employees should exemplify the strong, fit ideal of physical competence expected by their clients. Providing security meant going out and being strong, and the hacker-turned-security-expert, who spent his time staring at the multiple screens, was no exception.

But he wasn't the only one who had been slacking when it came to maintaining physical fitness. The other guys in the IT department had been getting soft in the gut as well.

Too much pizza.

Too much Gillen ice cream.

Too much computer time.

Easton was a vet, a kickass security specialist, and a fitness nut, and when nine of his thirty employees submitted for larger-sized uniforms, he just about blew his top.

Easton had announced a mandatory, company-wide triathlon during their annual holiday party, a thinly disguised appeal to their professional pride. Most of them put on a show of moaning and groaning, bitching over having to swim seven hundred and fifty, bike twelve miles, and run five kilometers in an August sixth city-sponsored race, but they had all eyed the list of prizes Easton revealed to sweeten the situation.

Terrible consequences would await those who failed to place with a respectable time, let alone those who failed to finish.

JESSE HAD mouthed off to Easton for doing this to him, but deep down he had recognized that it just might be for the best. A month of regular workouts had helped lift the gloom and solitary sorrow that breaking up with Renata had left behind. Jesse had dumped her when she'd become insufferable, driving him to finish his community college degree and work increasingly longer hours just so he could increase his social and financial standing. Until he accomplished that, her family would never accept him.

Her father, her overachieving brother, all of her educated, well-groomed cousins...

Jesse had hated what her family was doing to her – and to the two of them.

Just a break... to suck some air.

He stuck his head halfway out of the water, enjoying the way its warmth caressed him with every movement. The languid ease with which his long, black hair floated around him like tentacles.

As he turned his back to the lane, he saw an unexpected pair of shapely legs on the pool deck. Black tech shorts, a purple tee shirt matching black, purple-streaked hair that shone bright against the antiquated white-and-mint tile of the walls behind her. The color combination made her brown skin glow.

"Hey. You've been swimming every day this month." Her voice was melodious, touched by mischievous humor.

He grabbed the side of the pool and looked up at her.

"Yeah?"

"What's your name?"

"Jesse Hightower," he growled, suddenly self-conscious beneath her assessing look.

"I'm Yolanda," she said. "Jesse, I've been assigned to help you with your technique."

His eyes lit up. "Really? I just learned to swim four weeks ago."

"I know," she smirked. "It shows."

"Hey! It ain't my fault I never had the chance..."

"You're doing great, Jesse. Really," she said. "But I got some tricks up my sleeve that'll make it easier for you." She batted her eyelashes at him. "Will you let me show you?"

He flushed in embarrassment as she stripped off her t-shirt and shorts without waiting for his answer, slipping into the water next to him wearing nothing more than three triangles of purple cloth and some string.

Just for the sake of being polite, he let his gaze wander up and down her trim body. Not his type, really – too curvy, too female – but she'd been kind to offer her expertise.

She ignored his assessing look. "First, you need to learn how to breathe properly," she said. "Let's try an exercise, shall we?"

SEBASTIAN drifted to the end of his lane and stood chest-deep in the water. He reached for a sip of his custom-blended sports drink while throwing a covert glance at Yolanda and her newest student.

Yolanda had no shame, looking like a beach bunny in her little Brazilian getup. She was a trainer, and this was a serious pool where swimmers put in their time, focusing on technique rather than the scenery. She loved to irritate, though, and after years of training with him, she sure knew how to get his goat. She stripped and got in the water. It would ruin her hair for the day. She'd bitch about it, making it all his fault.

Hell, he might even point out that her hair was frizzier than usual. His thin lips curved in a faint smile. Anything to irritate Yolanda. At least she had made that poor man stop his incessant splashing.

He put his bottle on the pool deck and kicked off again, feeling the smooth caress of water flowing past his perfectly toned, waxed body. He relished the resistance as he dug his arm into the water in front of him, his hand plunging down, then continuing the stroke to his hip. Feeling the water, turning his palm and fingers just so to get more power, had become sheer instinct over the years. He kicked from the hip, smoothly and without making a sound. This was the feeling he craved – the peace and solitude of water as he propelled himself forward with efficiency and grace. The sounds of splashing and someone near-drowning from the other side of the pool had disappeared, neutralized by his personal trainer.

Only the air bubbles bursting by his ears disturbed his aquatic peace.

CHAPTER 2

JESSE CUT into the water before him with long, powerful arms. He went slowly. Each movement was deliberate, precise. Yolanda had begun to teach him this stroke several workouts ago and today – finally – it was all coming together into a smooth, controlled, almost effortless swim. The realization filled him with delighted surprise. He moved through the chlorinated water as fast as his former high-energy doggie paddle, but he felt a lot more relaxed. He even had breath to spare, which was a huge difference from hanging onto the end of the pool after every length, just to suck in some air.

His face broke through the surface on every other stroke, and always on the right side. Left side didn't want to work for him – not yet – as though his neck refused to crook far enough, water inundating his nose, his mouth.

At least I escaped the office.

Stupid Valentine's Day.

Hate it, hate it, hate it.

The disruptive thought invaded and his tempo slackened, which didn't make it possible for his head to emerge for a new gulp of air, which meant he had to flip onto his back into a safety float. He coughed hard, expelling the water he had accidentally inhaled.

So embarrassing.

Damn holiday's screwing up my workout.

Can't stand it.

He floated to the wall by the deep end and held onto the handle below the starting block. Ripping off his goggles, he let his eyes tear up. An almost-drowning coughing fit would do that. It had nothing to do with the dumb, red holiday or with Renata, who had loved it. She was long gone and good riddance, but he would have liked to have someone in his life to share the day with. He coughed again and dipped his head under, cleaning his face and, hopefully, his mind as well.

"EXCUSE ME," a quiet voice said next to him when he emerged. "Are you alright?"

Jesse turned. It was the fast guy from the other side of the pool. His skin was smooth and winter-pale—almost as white as his silicone swim cap—which made his gray, reflective goggles stand out in stark contrast. His thin lips looked like they should be blue with cold. Jesse glanced at the guy's mouth, wondering if the pink flush at the bow of his lips was a result of his recent interval training.

"Yeah. I just lost rhythm on my breathing. Thanks for asking." Jesse wiped his eyes with his wet hand. "By the way, thank you for sharing your trainer with me. She's really great."

"You're welcome." The guy floated two feet away, then flipped and quirked his eyebrow with a smile. "Why did you lose your rhythm?"

Jesse sighed and tilted his mane of wet hair back, letting it spread in the water behind him like ink.

"Just distracted, I guess." He paused. "I really, really hate Valentine's Day."

The other swimmer nodded, still treading water, and Jesse wondered how long he could stay afloat like that. "Women can be rather demanding."

"It used to be my favorite holiday. Renata used to love it…" Jesse trailed off.

"She's your girlfriend?"

"Was," Jesse said. "It's been over a year. You know, she was really wonderful while we were just friends, but then…" Jesse looked at the other swimmer. "I'm sorry. I didn't mean to spoil your workout with talk."

SEBASTIAN couldn't look away from the man's exotic features, let alone from the graceful veil of long hair in the water. His old coach would've killed anyone messing with the pool filters like that. A more experienced swimmer might've let his or her hair down for extra drag, however, the way Sebastian used to wear loose swim shirts for resistance workouts.

He let the stray thought pass in favor of responding. The new guy was a novice swimmer, and had been trying so hard. Making progress, too.

"I don't mind," Sebastian said. "We see one another almost every day in here. I'm glad Yolanda was able to help you with your technique."

Jesse grabbed the handhold under the starting block and braced his legs against the wall in a stretch. His extra flesh brimmed over the elastic of his swim trunks. He gave a painful exhale, then turned to face Sebastian again. "Is she coming today? I have a question for her."

Sebastian removed his goggles and set them at the edge of the pool. He propped his elbows on the edge and rubbed his eyes. The silicone seal had left a tangible impression around his eyes.

"Her husband's taking her out to lunch," he said. "For Valentine's Day, of course."

"Ah… I see." Disappointment passed over Jesse's tan face like a cloud, petering into patient resignation. "Oh, well."

"Maybe I could help," Sebastian offered. "If it's related to swimming, that is." He didn't mind sticking around. A fellow swimmer in need– it had nothing to do with those eyes, dark and deep, with a promise of warmth. Sharp cheekbones and straight nose set him apart from the run-of-the-mill men Sebastian saw every day. Was he Hispanic or Native? Maybe. Sebastian debated whether or not he should ask an invasive question like that.

Native American.

That term covered a lot of ground, but asking about a tribe sounded too weird. His Human Resources manager had impressed upon Sebastian the need to be "culturally sensitive," which he'd translated into meaning that he shouldn't ask questions at all.

Jesse interrupted his musings. "Really? Um... only if it's not too much trouble. I'm Jesse Hightower." They shook hands, trying to keep them on the surface of the chlorinated water. And Yolanda calls you Seb – is that your name?"

Sebastian froze at the sound of his loathed childhood nickname falling from the lips of a stranger, but then he restored his inner balance and nodded graciously. "Pleasure to meet you, Jesse. I'm Sebastian, but you may use my nickname, if you wish." His lips turned up in the slightest hint of a smile.

SEBASTIAN had thought the man's surname had sounded somewhat familiar. Now he knew his given name, and that, together with his singular appearance and his sister's name on Jesse's lips, completed the picture of the stranger's identity.

This, then, was the elusive and controversial Jesse Hightower.

His sister's former boyfriend.

The man whose background was so dire, his appearance so startling, and his education so lacking that he had never been introduced to the rest of the family. Renata, as Sebastian recalled, had met him during one of her volunteer projects, the one that helped former juvenile delinquents study for their GED exams. This meant Jesse had been a high school dropout. According to Yolanda, however, he was currently employed by 11th Hour Security Company as one of their computer experts.

A sudden wave of curiosity rose inside his chest and he made an immediate decision to keep his identity as Renata's brother secret. He justified his subterfuge as kindness. Why not be secretive if the other swimmer found the topic a painful one?

"What do you need help with, Jesse?"

"I keep almost-drowning when I try to breathe on my left."

Sebastian paused, then nodded. "Oh. Let's see you do it, then."

THEY WALKED to the locker rooms in companionable silence. Jesse reached up high to turn on the old-fashioned, communal showers and was surprised to see Sebastian strip his Spandex knee-length swimsuit along with his swim cap.

"Oh… sorry," Sebastian said. "There is one private shower stall around the corner. I take it you're not used to these?"

Jesse shrugged, feigning nonchalance. "It's been a while. We used to take group showers after soccer practice. It didn't used to be such a big deal." Jesse had never felt comfortable in group showers – not ever since he discovered his body was wired along equal-opportunity lines when it came to men and women.

Sebastian was hot.

Last thing Jesse needed was embarrassing himself by sprouting wood.

He untied the string of his long, loose swim trunks and tossed them on the wet tile floor with Sebastian's, studying the fascinating layout of mint-green tiles on the shower floor. Time to focus on the task of cleaning up. On the tile patterns. On anything but the man next to him.

The tiles went row by row.

Shampoo.

Column by column.

Conditioner.

"Um, could I please use your conditioner?"

Jesse jerked his head up, trying not to panic. He avoided eye contact, but try as he might, it was impossible not to catch a glimpse of Sebastian's lovely, athletic body lines. He'd hate for things to get awkward. "Uh? Sure."

He passed the bottle over, noting the way Sebastian's lats stood out as he raised his hands to treat his short blond hair.

Fucking gorgeous.

Sebastian returned the bottle with a gracious nod. "Thanks. Chlorine needs to be fought at every step."

SEBASTIAN observed Jesse on the sly. Taller than him and broader in the shoulders, he had serious love handles and a bit of a beer belly. His otherwise fine musculature was disguised under an even layer of insulation. He carried his extra weight well enough on his large frame, but still – what had Renata ever seen in him? She'd always been very particular about the outward appearance of her boyfriends. There was the hair—no doubt a spectacular asset—and the tattoo of some kind of a totem and a bird on his left shoulder blade wrapped to his shoulder and upper arm in an exotic and almost tribal design.

Maybe the weight gain had been recent? She had cried for days afterward, so she must have had strong feelings for him.

Sebastian finished up and stepped out from under the stream of water, aware that he was being a tad judgmental.

Maybe Jesse was nice.

Maybe it was all that lovely inside.

Maybe it was his striking facial structure and the promise of strength that had appealed to his sister.

Sebastian realized Jesse could be gorgeous – but he was his sister's ex, and Sebastian had no business thinking of him that way. He censored his thoughts and walked to his locker to dry off in a routine, harmonious dance inherent to swimmers who used the most efficient system of getting dry and dressed possible as quickly as possible.

Jesse wasn't far behind him. Sebastian watched him pull on loose, black jeans and an oversized polo shirt emblazoned with The 11th Hour Security Company's logo. The garment hung over his waist in a strategic effort to disguise his excess padding.

A sudden pang of empathy seized Sebastian's heart. It was hard to start swimming from scratch, and this man had lasted a whole six weeks. His fortitude was commendable.

Along with empathy came curiosity. Sebastian, an intensely

private individual when it came to his own affairs, was like a curious cat in regards to his younger sister's life. She seemed to have been serious about this man—they'd known each other for years. A sudden, burning desire awoke in his heart to discover what had happened.

Fastening his blue silk tie, he remembered that his large house would be empty that night, as Renata would be out with Paul. Jesse, quite probably, had no social engagements. A sudden, brazen thought rampaged through his mind.

"Jesse."

"Yeah?" He was seated on a bench, working a hairbrush through yard-long tresses, his strokes short and methodical.

"I have nothing scheduled for tonight. Would you care to join me for dinner?"

Jesse looked up and froze, taking in Sebastian's metamorphosis from wet swimmer to elegant businessman.

Sebastian bit back a smile. He knew he looked good. His black, polished shoes gripped the wet locker room tile floor as he slipped his arms into the sleeves of his fitted suit jacket. His hair, darkened to brown with trapped moisture, was slicked to the sides where it would dry into obedient spikes and waves. He knew he looked nothing like the swimmer Jesse spoke with only ten minutes ago.

"Me? Really? Don't you think we'll just be supporting the industry in their delusion that the so-called 'V-day' is, in fact, a holiday of significance?"

Sebastian inclined his head just a fraction, turning his narrow lips up in a faint smile.

"If you don't mind crossing most of Pittsburgh, there is this little hole-in-the-wall Chinese restaurant in Oakland I like. It's likely to be half-empty. It's the student ghetto, so wear your sloppiest clothes. No need to stand out in that neighborhood."

Sebastian was satisfied to see a glint of excitement in the other man's eyes.

JESSE was awed.

He didn't think much of the Audi sedan Sebastian drove – a car was just a car. He could save up for one, if he really cared to do so. He wasn't awed by Sebastian's fancy-ass business suit he'd worn earlier, or by his obvious position of authority which came through in the way he carried himself..

None of that mattered.

Sebastian was fascinating because he possessed skills.

Discipline.

Knowledge.

He was an athlete in prime physical condition – just like Jesse had strived to be three years ago. But then he had let himself go, almost drowning in the morass of worthlessness and depression that had filled him back then. He flinched, remembering the cause of it.

"C'mon, Renata. Just one more kiss."

Renata gazed at him, her blue eyes calm and calculating. "You're such an enticing, fascinating man. So much potential. And I've done so much for you already, Jesse." She licked her lips. "I enjoy investing in you. Helping you. But if you want us to be together and meet my family, well...."

Jesse's jaw tightened, hoping Renata wouldn't go on one of her tirades against her demanding father and snobbish brother. He didn't want to hear any more about "investing in himself," or about the way her father and her brother despised the unwashed, uneducated masses.

He just wanted to be with her. The two of them, alone, sharing the little things in their lives. Instead of enjoying life and smelling the roses, Renata stressed over not bringing a mere GED student into the house. A high school dropout who'd fended for himself on the streets would never do – if he wanted to be welcome in the Gillen mansion he'd heard so much about, he had to at least finish his college degree.

"How did you do on your calculus midterm, Jesse?"

"I'm not here to discuss calculus..." His lean, muscled arm snaked across her back as he leaned his chiseled face toward her. "Well? Do I get one?"

"Only if you got an A, Jesse. You know the rules."

He bit back a groan of frustration. His arm slipped off her shoulders, yielding to the laws of gravity unopposed. His grade was eighty-nine points out of a hundred. He had missed his kiss by only one percentage point.

He was never good enough, and never would be.

SEBASTIAN parked his car in a garage nine blocks away, deciding that they could walk to the restaurant.

"Thanks for picking me up, Seb," Jesse said. "I'm afraid it would've been difficult the other way around."

"Oh?" Sebastian asked, no longer flinching at the use of his nickname. He had, after all, allowed it.

"Yeah…I bike everywhere. I'd have to ask you to get your bike out of winter storage and pull your gloves on."

"You bike." He evaluated the concept with compressed lips, tasted it, tried it on for size. "Even in the winter?"

"Oh yeah." Jesse looked each way before they crossed Atwood Street.

Sebastian paused and looked around. The air was still winter-dry, and the bare trees that grew out of the squares of earth in the sidewalk were far from showing signs of life. "I had to start training right away, so I sold the car. It was too tempting to just drive, you know? This way, I don't have a choice. If I really need one, I use one of those downtown car-sharing programs."

"I assume when you need to go shopping?"

"Yeah." Jesse grinned. "I have baskets on the bike, but that's just for a few groceries."

"Amazing. How far is it for you?" Sebastian asked.

There was no mistaking the enthusiasm in Jesse's voice and the glee in his expression. "Oh, about five miles each way. Not too bad. From North Side to the Strip District? It used to take me forty-five minutes, but by now I've shaved it to about half an hour. Much depends on traffic, of course. And on how much stuff I carry back."

Sebastian nodded. He stretched his stride to avoid a cracked part of a sidewalk the tree roots heaved into a speedbump. A car passed, slow and on the prowl, probably looking for a parking space. "Yolanda told me you're training for a triathlon. Something about a company policy?"

Jesse only growled.

Sebastian smiled at Jesse's show of temper. "You are fortunate. I have never learned to ride a bicycle."

Jesse slid his eyes toward Sebastian, amazed. "Never? How come?"

"Overprotective family," Sebastian shrugged. "They thought I'd get kidnapped. I rode horses instead. Mostly just as cross-training to complement my swimming. Dressage is highly demanding, however, and I had to choose between the two."

"You gave up riding?" Jesse's voice was incredulous. He'd ridden in his early teens, back out West. Once he'd entered the foster care system off the reservation, however, his riding opportunities had dried up. Giving up any chance to get up on a horse was inconceivable.

"Pools are more accessible than stables. At least I can still swim."

Jesse's keen ear didn't fail to detect the bitter note in Sebastian's voice.

SEBASTIAN ground to a halt in front of a glass door in a brick facade, and Jesse stopped and looked at him with a questioning gaze. The sign on the door advertised Cuban sandwiches, and there was something Chinese-sounding right above it.

"Come in," Sebastian said as he opened the door and held it for Jesse. "It's upstairs."

"Huh." Jesse let the door shut behind them, keeping the February chill outside. Warmth spread through him as soon as he could smell the pungent mixture of exotic spices.

"You weren't kidding about the 'hole-in-the-wall' part," Jesse said. They walked up scuffed, vinyl-covered stairs that opened into a long and narrow room full of cheap tables and chairs. Three families, all Asian, were tucked in at the round tables in the corner, but the place was empty otherwise. A middle-aged Asian woman nodded a warm hello. "Two?"

"Two," Sebastian confirmed. Jesse inhaled again, tasting the fragrant air, as he followed them to a table in the middle of the room. Sebastian shrugged out of his fleece-lined denim jacket. A wine-colored turtleneck warded off the February chill and looked a bit dressier for this place than what Jesse chose to wear. He reminded himself this wasn't a date as he hung his leather jacket next to Sebastian's and slid into the booth opposite him.

"So what's good?"

"Everything. I come here for the spice. This is the only place in town that makes their food hot enough for me."

A WAITER came out with two waters, two cups, a pot of hot tea and two plastic-covered menus that had seen better days.

Sebastian scanned the familiar selection and chose spicy pork intestines and Szechuan eggplant. "You can get real, authentic Chinese dishes here," he said. "See, they even divided the menu into an American part and a Chinese part. They didn't used to have the Chinese part translated."

Jesse looked over recipes that didn't waste any part of an animal's body. "Lamb kidneys? Cow stomach? Seriously?" He didn't look put off, merely intrigued.

"Seriously. I've tried it, it's... interesting."

The amused glance Jesse threw him made Sebastian determined to have Jesse try one of these oddball dishes another day.

"I'll go with Kung Pao Chicken. Mild."

No surprise there. Before his trips to China, Sebastian would have probably chosen the same thing.

"So, what company do you work for?" Jesse asked while they waited for their wonton soup.

"The Gillen Frozen Desserts Company."

"No way! That's my favorite ice cream!"

"Really," Sebastian said, assessing.

"Yep. Although I had to give it up. It's evil. Totally addictive, as I'm sure you know." Jesse grinned. "So what's your favorite flavor?"

Sebastian looked into those warm, dark eyes, feeling a sudden pang of guilt.

"I don't eat the stuff. In fact, I dislike sweets."

"So…" Jesse rubbed his neck in momentary confusion. "So why do you work there, if you don't like it?"

Sebastian twirled his beer bottle between his long fingers. "I don't have much choice."

Jesse took a sip of his beer as he processed the answer.

"You don't sound as though you like your job very much, Seb," he said, his voice serious.

"I don't." The admission surprised Sebastian. Not liking his work at Gillen was a closely held secret.

"So quit!"

Sebastian sighed. "It's complicated."

Jesse was just about to object – from Jesse's expression, situations were either good or bad – when their soup and main dishes arrived at the same time, providing respite from questioning.

"I hope it won't be too spicy for you," Sebastian said with a slight smirk.

"I'll manage."

It was hot – apparently even mild was on the edge of Jesse's comfort zone – but manage he did.

"SO I JUST wanted to know how you do it," Jesse asked. "How do you keep in shape if your job is almost as sedentary as mine?"

"First, I don't eat the ice cream," Sebastian said in a dry voice. Jesse's eyes glanced up fast enough to notice the upturned hint of a smile.

Ah, a joke.

He laughed.

"You sound like a drug dealer who knows better." Jesse's voice faltered as he saw a mask of guilt cover Sebastian's previously content expression.

"I'm lactose-intolerant. Besides, you can do the same," Sebastian pointed out.

"Easy for you to say," Jesse said. "The stuff makes you sick. I wish I was lactose-intolerant, too."

"So, Jesse…" Sebastian worked hard to recover, not wanting to ruin the mood. "If you don't mind me asking – you were lean and athletic once. Am I correct?"

Jesse nodded, sipping more water.

"So what happened?"

A long beat of silence, then Jesse answered. "Renata happened."

Sebastian noted Jesse's much quieter voice, his subdued expression. This was Sebastian's sister they were talking about. He knew he was crossing a line, not letting Jesse know who he was in the grander scheme of things.

He yearned to know what happened, both to Renata, and to Jesse. "Your former girlfriend?"

"My former best friend. She pushed and pushed. For my own good, I'm sure." Jesse raised his gaze to meet Sebastian's. His expression exuded misery.

"She pushed," Sebastian echoed.

Few bites of food, a sigh. "She was a relentless perfectionist," Jesse finally said. "I started skipping soccer and karate to hold down a job and go to school at night, then wound up having to look for a better job—something to satisfy her. There was a lot of stress…" He sipped some ice water, looking like he was gathering his thoughts, buying extra time, then continued.

Sebastian nodded and sipped his own ice water, mirroring Jesse. His sister could be a pill. He knew that firsthand. But she always meant well.

"Her family was really demanding, I guess. Her older brother sounded like a real asshole."

Ice water went down the wrong tube.

Sebastian coughed, grabbing a napkin to cover his mouth. "Sorry," he whispered. He was, after all, the asshole Jesse was talking about.

"But I loved her," Jesse continued. "I loved her, so I did it for her. But it never ended, y'know? She was never happy enough. Then I had to get even better grades – so that they would find me acceptable. I was never good enough, Seb. Never, from the very beginning."

Sebastian knew.

Not much was ever good enough for his sister.

Jesse finished the water in his glass. "I think she loved me once, but then I became just another salvage project to her. I used to have my own dreams…" Jesse's trailed off.

He used to be good with cars. Working with his hands had always given him pleasure, yet he had switched from cars to computer maintenance because it was, according to Renata, "higher class."

Higher class my ass.

"DEPRESSED?"

Jesse realized he had allowed to let his expression sag. He looked up and pasted on a smile in an effort to reset the mood, but he failed to stop his deep sigh.

He cleared his throat. "Only the last three years. Although, as much as I owe her for helping me, breaking up with her was the best thing I've ever done for myself."

Sebastian nodded. Renata was a perfectionist and nothing was ever shiny enough. No one was ever accomplished enough. He had seen her subject her current boyfriend to scathing barbs for the smallest of infractions.

"So, what's your goal?"

Jesse laughed out loud. He looked Sebastian up and down, making him feel vaguely self-conscious.

"My goal is to beat you."

Sebastian started. "Beat me how? And why?"

"Someday, I'll beat you in a race. A swim race. If it's really just a matter of learnin' the right form and working at it, then I can do that." He grinned. "As to the reason why… "

Jesse paused, and Sebastian leaned forward.

"Even though you hate your job, you still manage to find happiness in the other things that you do."

Sebastian sat still, staring at Jesse and the way his sleek, raven hair shone, bound into a tidy ponytail.

Such a simple goal.

It occurred to him that his sister was a fool.

CHAPTER 3

JESSE WOKE to the third blaring of his alarm, fuzzy-headed and congested. Everything seemed a bit off-kilter in the still
darkness of his bedroom and, suddenly, the thought of immersing
himself in a cold pool sent a shiver through his body.

He groaned. Coming down with a cold was the worst possible
thing that could happen to him. It had only been one month since
Yolanda had taken an interest in him, yet he'd improved enough
to swim four hundred meters during his lunch hour and still have
enough time to stretch out, shower, and dress. His improvement
was remarkable.

Too bad he didn't feel like doing anything today.

Staying in bed sounded fabulous.

He could call in sick. Take a day off. Sleep himself out, catch up
on his email–...

He rolled out of bed and landed barefoot on the cheap apartment rug. The familiar scratch of rough fiber against the soles of
his feet woke him up enough to haul himself to his feet and lumber
to the bathroom. He pissed, shrugged off shorts and t-shirt, then
stepped on the scale.

WOW. Like, really?

Standing under the shower, letting the steam from the hot
water soften the gunk in his sinuses, he pondered the fact that

the numbers on the scale had finally budged. That finally, he had reached the milestone of losing fifteen pounds since the beginning of January. That was five pounds a month. Not a huge amount – but he'd also been lifting weights twice a week, and was gaining back some of his previous muscle mass, too.

THERE WAS no way he was going to skip work now, and no way he was going to skip his pool workout. Seb would be there… to the best of Jesse's knowledge, he never skipped, either. Ever. Jesse's weight was one quarter of the way to where he wanted it to be, and that meant he could get his reward now – he could open the big, flat box stashed away under his bed. After work, he would come home, pull out his tools, and assemble the new bike he had bought himself as a special treat in anticipation of reaching one of his goals.

Breakfast proved to be difficult territory. Since Jesse was so emotionally riled over finally having reached a certain number, he wanted to celebrate. And how else does one celebrate if not with food? Pancakes. With syrup. Or maybe a slice of an apple pie with caramel sauce–but only one slice. Floating on cloud nine over his weight loss, he figured he'd pick it up from the diner that was along his route to work. He would, after all, swim it off later.

His stomach clenched with hunger pangs as he watched the three girls and two boys eat. He was the only foster kid who wasn't allowed dinner. He'd rather starve than service his foster-father's "important acquaintance".

Jesse's last foster-mother had been an old, kind and generous woman who had always encouraged him in anything he endeavored. His passion for soccer was equal to his passion for the special treat she provided: Gillen Chocolate Ice Cream and home-baked cookies. Grandma—as she liked to be called—would never have forced him to spend time with a stranger, let alone spend the whole night with them. But then she had broken her hip, and Youth Services had sent him to this group home.

"Don't even think about it, Hightower," Kerrick said as Jesse glanced longingly at the padlocked refrigerator and pantry. *"You know the rules. You work, you eat. You don't work... well, let's see how long you can hold out."*

Jesse shook the memory off like a bad dream. Thinking about those days – those best-forgotten days – always made him hungry. Unreasonably so. He could eat and eat, and yet he'd still feel Kerrick's cold hazel eyes on him, accompanied by the yawning pit of deprivation, followed closely by the eerie, light-headed sensation that would precede his passing out for the night.

He fished his cell phone out of his pocket and found the number Sebastian had entered there only two weeks ago. He'd had no cause to contact him, not until today. He chose to text. It was less personal.

JESSE: *Are you up yet?*

He cracked two eggs into a bowl, added a dash of water, and whisked them with a fork. A small non-stick pan was preheating on the stove, seasoned with a few drops of olive oil.

Just as he poured the egg mixture into the hot pan, his phone beeped, announcing the arrival of a new text message. Jesse put down the empty bowl, he wiped his hands on a kitchen towel and picked up his phone, swiping the screen with his thumb to unlock it—picking up a spatula with his other hand to tend to his eggs.

SEB: *Good morning, Jesse! What's up?*

Jesse stirred his eggs with one hand as he read the message, and a slow smile blossomed on his face. The eggs were about done. He moved the pan, letting the residual heat finish them off, while he put a whole-wheat tortilla over the hot burner to toast, and rapidly typed out is reply:

JESSE: *Reached a weight goal. Wanna be BAD to celebrate.*

Assembling his breakfast burrito—adding a few tiny drops of Tabasco, which barely rated as hot sauce in Sebastian's book—he grabbed a glass from the cabinet and poured a glass of water, setting it down next to his waiting cup of coffee. He didn't have long to wait for Seb's reply.

SEB: *Don't sabotage yourself. You won't beat me if you do.*

Jesse grimaced. Of course Sebastian had to go and remind him of his ill-considered words! He bit off some of his breakfast, texting back:

JESSE: *I might have a cold. Was thinking about skipping the pool today?*

Seb's answer came quickly:

SEB: *"Yeah. Just quit. Make it easy for me; I thought of blowing off today as well."*

Jesse rolled his eyes at Sebastian's obvious attempt at reverse psychology, but his words had an impact. He couldn't just quit. He'd come so far in just three months.

JESSE: *OK. I'll swim if you swim. It's always easier with a friend.*

SEBASTIAN stared at his cell phone screen, speechless.

'It's always easier with a friend.'

He shut the screen off and slipped the slim rectangle into his suit pocket. A small hint of a smile tugged at his lips as he reached for his car keys.

"What is it, Sebastian?" Renata emerged in her yoga pants and a sports bra, ready to tackle a new routine in her own personal search for perfection. He let his smile linger.

"Oh, just good news. From a friend."

"Oh good! I bet the stockholders will be ecstatic, whatever it is! Who was it? Emille? Or Joselyn?"

"Neither," Sebastian replied as he schooled his face into a mask of distracted morning chaos. He couldn't possibly mention Jesse.

As he motored to the office park with other commuters, his mind kept replaying that magic word over and over.

Friend… Friend… Friend…

He didn't make friends easily, nor did he retain them very well. There were sycophants aplenty, trying to inveigle themselves into his good graces, hoping for a job or business contacts or a lucrative marriage. When he had been invited to birthday parties as a boy, it had inevitably been to the houses of his family's business associates, where he had been forced to interact with spoiled brats when he would have much rather stay at home and read. In retaliation, he had walled himself off, building up a defensive barrier against their so-called 'friendship', ready to launch a preemptive strike at the least threat of breach.

Jesse, however, had nothing to gain from him, other than simple camaraderie.

Once again a faint smile flitted across Sebastian's lips as he prepared to start his workday.

A friend.

THEY HAD finished their swim for the day. Jesse was glad he'd shown up. Yolanda had praised him for his improvement and berated Sebastian for swimming like an old lady.

"I always strive to emulate you," Sebastian had answered in a serious, dry voice. Jesse, who had been drinking from his bottle at the time, just about choked—both at Sebastian's comeback and at Yolanda's answering irate expression.

Dried off, dressed, and ready to return to their respective jobs, Sebastian cleared his throat.

"Ah, Jesse," he began. "Congratulations again. Looks like you're going to need to go clothes shopping."

Jesse grinned, gleaming teeth flashing. "Well, going to Goodwill for new pants is one way of celebrating, I guess."

"Why buy second-hand?" Sebastian asked. The tension around his eyes betrayed distress to Jesse's observant eye.

"Why not?" he answered. "I won't need that size for long, anyway. Why waste money?"

Sebastian slid through the glass door, nodding his thanks at Jesse for holding it open for him. "There must be a better way to celebrate."

"Hmmm… maybe you could help me, then." Jesse said.

"I'm not buying you a cake, Jesse. Or bringing you any ice cream," Sebastian said.

"No, nothing like that… just, I have something to show you," Jesse answered, failing to suppress an excited grin. "Can you meet me after work tomorrow? At the City Gardens Park?"

Sebastian thought for a minute, mentally flipping through his schedule. Friday night, no engagements – why not? He nodded.

"Great! Oh, and wear something casual."

"Like, not a tuxedo?" Sebastian teased, and Jesse rolled his eyes.

"Like, sweatpants, you fuckin' wiseass."

"Jesse." Sebastian's tone was reproachful, but he was fighting a smile.

"Sorry, sorry," Jesse said, holding up his hands in surrender. "But you're gonna love this, I promise!"

The big-kid grin on Jesse's face was contagious, and Sebastian found his mouth curve up gently in response, warmth spreading all the way up to his eyes.

He'd found a friend who made him smile, and didn't want anything in return. There was a first time for everything.

JESSE GOT home from work twenty minutes early that Friday, wolfed down a turkey sandwich, and changed. Half an hour later, he was waiting by the park entrance. He wore biking shorts under his sweat pants. He wore bike shoes on his feet, too. They looked much like flat sneakers, but their sole contained a metal clip, which allowed him to "clip in" into his bicycle's pedals. That way, the efficiency of every stroke would be increased by approximately thirty percent, engaging not only the quadriceps when pushing the pedal down, but also the hamstrings when pulling the pedal up. Or so he had read on various triathlon websites.

The new bike, purchased on sale at Roadbikeoutlet.com, was his reward. His old bike stood right next to it, looking stodgy and slow by comparison. A regular mountain bike with decent cushioning and fat tires, decent for jumping curbs while dodging traffic, but not high-end enough for jumping logs on forested trails.

He waited.

And waited.

Jesse began to fret, and he had almost reached for his phone when a familiar figure floated into view. There was Sebastian, smiling and cheerful and looking good enough to eat. He was dressed in a gray Yale sweatshirt, black sweatpants, and running shoes.

Jesse stood and waved to attract his attention.

AFTER HE parked his Audi and locked it, Sebastian sauntered to the park's entrance. He hadn't visited this verdant gem in many years. Crowns of majestic oaks and sycamores promised to shade the asphalt paths once their leaves have emerged. Now, after six in the evening, the lack of canopy allowed what little light there was left to make the path feel rather private and mysterious. Jesse was supposed to be waiting somewhere nearby.

Sebastian drew a deep breath, enjoying the cold, earthy smell of last year's decaying leaves. Jesse was generally prompt, but Sebastian didn't see him. When he was about to reach for his phone, a shape detached itself from a tree-trunk in the faltering light of the day. Relief flooded through him when he recognized Jesse, and the other man lifted his hand in a wave of greeting.

Sebastian walked over, wondering in what manner he was to help his…friend…celebrate his achievement.

"Hey, Sebastian! What kept you?"

"It's hard to find parking in this neighborhood," he answered. He was fifteen minutes late.

"Ah." Jesse nodded. "That's why I bike. And now, you can too!"

Sebastian followed the gesture of his large hand toward the two bicycles. One rested on a kick-stand. The other, a sleek machine of black and red, was propped against a tree.

He drew in a breath and allowed it to settle, calming his nerves before he trusted himself with a reaction. "Jesse. You know I do not know how to ride a bicycle."

"Sebastian." Jesse was emulating his own serious tone. "I didn't know how to swim until two and a half months ago."

Sebastian shrugged. "It's kind of you to want to share this with me, but…"

"Fine then, just go ahead and quit without even tryin'!"

Sebastian nearly flinched at the harshness of Jesse's tone, the mockery in his voice a new side to his friend that he hadn't been expecting. He sounded a lot like Renata—apparently Jesse had learned more from Sebastian's sister than just how to be a better student.

He faced Jesse, who loomed over him under the gnarled cathedral of sycamore branches, refusing to be bullied or intimidated.

"Jesse Hightower, that was completely uncalled for," he said in his sternest boardroom voice. "I will give it a try, but I do not promise to like it. Normally I wouldn't even do that, especially not after you tried to goad me into it, but we are here to celebrate your accomplishment."

JESSE HAD taken a gamble in cajoling the quiet, laid-back man, and it had paid off. Sebastian had been close to walking away, but hadn't. His tone had been stern and unyielding, and Jesse was suddenly reminded of the steel that had always been Renata's core. Disconcerted by the notion, he shook it off and handed Sebastian a bicycling helmet.

"Here, you should probably wear this."

Sebastian eased the headgear on without protest, though he did manage to convey his distaste for the whole endeavor with thinly-pressed lips as he buckled and adjusted the helmet's straps.

"All right, then. We both have some learning to do," Jesse said, once he was sure Sebastian was listening. "You need to learn to ride a regular bike, and I need to learn to ride this racing bike."

"Are they that different?" Sebastian eyed the two machines with curiosity, his earlier annoyance seeming to disappear. Jesse hid a smile.

"Oh yeah," he answered, then launched into an explanation. "Yours is about four times the weight of mine. It has an aluminum frame and wide wheels, it's cushioned, and it can jump small obstacles if you know how. The handlebars are farther apart for better balance. The front has a disc brake so that you can still stop even when it's raining." Jesse stroked the handlebars of his utility bike with affection. It had gotten him where he needed to go for years. He shook off his nostalgia to continue his explanation.

"Now on this new bike, look at the way the handlebars curve under." He indicated the sweep with one hand, glancing up to see if Sebastian was following along. The other man seemed to be listening attentively, so Jesse kept going. "These are aero-bars on top; on long rides I can rest my elbows."

Sebastian nodded, eyes tracking the movement of Jesse's hand as he pointed out different features. He tapped the tires with his fingers. "See the wheels? Very thin and light, larger than the tires on the other bike. The system has a lot less friction resistance. It has fewer gears than the mountain bike to reduce its weight, and the best part is, the body's made of carbon fiber."

"It looks expensive," Sebastian said after long moments in which he examined the bike thoroughly, going so far as to walk around it to take it all in. Jesse was having trouble trying to fight down his smile—he'd definitely caught the other man's interest.

"It was," he answered the unspoken question. "I sold my car, remember? I can buy three racing bikes with the money I got for it."

Sebastian's eyebrows lifted fractionally, and Jesse rubbed the back of his neck self-consciously. "Don't look at me like that— sometimes when you want to make an omelet, you gotta break a few eggs."

Not giving the other man a chance to comment, Jesse adjusted the seat height on the mountain bike. "Now, you ride horses, right? So, you know about balance, I guess?"

"Equitation is all about balance and control," Sebastian answered, his eyes focused on the way Jesse's hands were holding the handlebars.

"Good," he said, not asking about the unfamiliar word. He figured it had something to do with horses and left it at that. "Just pretend you're riding a really skinny horse, then. And remember, the faster you go, the more stable you are."

"Simple physics," Sebastian said in a dry voice.

"Right! Exactly!" He held the bike steady with one hand, gesturing for the other man to come close. Sebastian slung a long leg over, settled his weight on the seat, and grasped the handlebars. Jesse gave him an assessing look. "Grab the breaks and squeeze them until you're ready to go."

Only when Sebastian leaned on the breaks, Jesse left him perched, balanced precariously on his old mountain bike, and went to retrieve his own new baby. "So I want you to just coast on the bike. We'll go down this path, which is a nice, easy ride." He pointed at the brakes mounted to the handlebars. "You're squeezing the brakes now. That's to slow down or stop. You let go, the bike will go."

"What are these?" Sebastian asked, indicating the smaller levers on top of the handlebars.

"The gears. Don't worry about those for now. You go first, and I'll follow."

They set off, Jesse coasting, balancing on his narrower and less stable racing bike right behind Sebastian, whose legs were outstretched to the sides, almost dragging his toes on the asphalt, touching this or that side occasionally.

Not too much later, Sebastian decided to try pedaling. The park's paths had been abandoned with the failing of the light and the cold and damp late-winter air begun to creep under their clothes.

An attentive student, Sebastian started pedaling faster, working hard on maintaining his balance.

Jesse managed to clip into the pedals of his racing bike, following him with silent, effortless stealth.

They followed the path for a good five minutes and just when Jesse began to feel great about Sebastian's unexpected skill, he saw him waver and jerk to the side.

A fallen branch blocked the path, barely visible in the twilight gloom.

"Use your brakes!" Jesse shouted, not knowing if Sebastian could hear him. Alarmed, he saw Sebastian right his course and pedal even faster, accelerating toward the obstacle.

"Seb! No!"

Jesse powered up his cadence, catching up to Sebastian just as he yanked the handlebars up, his front wheel clearing the six-inch tree limb. Jesse pumped his brakes and skidded to a stop, unwilling to jump or crash his new and somewhat delicate carbon fiber bike.

Sebastian also stopped.

That is, his front wheel cleared the obstacle but, unlike a horse, the rear of his steed didn't follow automatically.

His bicycle stopped.

Following the inevitable Newtonian laws of motion, Sebastian's momentum remained conserved, and he continued on his original trajectory, ejected from his seat. He flew across the handlebars and half-tucked himself before his body skidded across the black asphalt path.

Jesse had already abandoned his own bike, leaping the branch and running to the motionless figure on the ground.

"Sebastian! Seb, are you all right?"

SEBASTIAN lay stunned on the ground. He knew not to move abruptly after a fall; it was important to assess the damage. He tentatively wiggled his toes, then his fingers. There was no undue pain or numbness in his neck or back.

Gentle hands touched his shoulders.

"Sebastian."

Jesse's worried face shoved into view, and Sebastian groaned, cautiously pushing himself upright.

He sat up. "I'm okay, Jesse," he said, waving off the other man's hand. He was—just a bit banged up.

"No you're not!" Jesse ground out. "You're a mess."

Sebastian sighed. "My neck's not broken. I'm not paralyzed. It's no worse than falling off a horse."

He looked into the hot, glistening eyes of Jesse Hightower, who knelt on the ground beside him.

"Fuck, Seb, you weren't moving and I figured…you know…"

Still moving carefully, he rose to his feet and cautiously stretched his back. "I was just checking the damage, Jesse."

Everything seemed to be in working order—though he was going to be very sore later—and he glanced over at his companion, who had also risen to his feet and was watching him like a hawk. He dusted himself off. "Well, back in the saddle!" he said.

He then eyed the fallen bike. "Although, I must say, your horse is rather deficient at jumping obstacles."

"Seb," Jesse said repressively, rubbing at his face, failing to be discreet about wiping away suspicious moisture. "Didya know you're bleeding?"

Sebastian stopped and looked at his hands. The outside of his right palm had suffered a minor abrasion. "It's nothing."

"I'm talkin' 'bout yer face," Jesse said forcefully, laying a hand on the other man's shoulder, slipping into the harsh slang of his younger years. Sebastian turned to face him. The coffee-colored eyes were fraught with worry and a warm, gentle finger wiped moisture off his cheek.

Sebastian flinched at the sudden stab of pain.

"Sorry." Jesse's finger ran up to the outside of his eye, then above it. "Take off your helmet," he said.

Sebastian complied, only to have the slightly taller man peer at his forehead, his fingers probing, causing more stinging pain.

"There's a gash in your forehead, running to the outside of your eyebrow. It's bleeding pretty bad…you might need stitches."

Sebastian raised his own fingers to his face. The wetness that he had thought was just sweat was, in fact, red and sticky, and left a mess all over his hand.

"Shit," he said, letting the word slip out. Dazed at the knowledge that he was bleeding, he forgot to guard his tongue "I can't go home like this. Renata's going to kill me."

JESSE COULDN'T believe his ears. The other man had uttered a swear-word, and then said the last name he had ever expected to hear.

"Sebastian…" he began cautiously, "There's a Renata in your family?"

He trained his eyes on his friend, who suddenly averted his gaze, looking down and away.

Renata wasn't exactly a common name, and combined with the way Sebastian was avoiding his gaze, Jesse knew he was right to be suspicious.

"Sebastian?" he prompted, hoping that he was wrong.

A look of guilty misery joined the streaks of crimson blood on Sebastian's face as he looked at Jesse, then straightened fully—less imposing-businessman and more prisoner-on-his-way-to-his-execution.

"I'm sorry, Jesse. I was hoping you'd never find out," Sebastian, his friend, said quietly.

Jesse knew his shock and dismay—and yeah, his betrayal—was written all over his face, his eyebrows slamming down in a frown.

"What's your last name, Sebastian?" he demanded.

"I am Sebastian Gillen. Seb is merely my childhood nickname. Which I loathe, by the way."

Jesse stepped back, away from Sebastian, his eyes widening as he confirmed his suspicions.

Gillen. As in Renata Gillen." he said, and Sebastian nodded. "What, so, you're like her cousin or something?"

Sebastian shook his head.

"No? Then…her brother?"

Sebastian nodded, misery shading his handsome face.

"You…YOU! You're the pain-in-the-ass older brother! You're the one who'd made my life miserable for how many years now?"

Jesse kept staggering backward as he spoke, gesticulating in wild gestures, not looking where he was going.

The very branch that Sebastian had failed to jump on his first-ever bike ride now brought an abrupt halt to Jesse's retreat, tripping him. He fell, his arms flailing in a vain effort to catch himself, and his left forearm struck the heavy metal teeth of the forgotten bike's pedal.

Fabric and skin ripped.

"Ow, fuck!" Jesse howled, fighting the pain and frustration of his injuries without Sebastian's stoic aplomb.

Sebastian came over and handed him his hand, pulling him back to his feet.

"Are you okay?" Sebastian's voice was quiet and composed, just the way it had been when he had addressed him at the pool for the very first time.

Their eyes met, and Jesse knew that his face reflected every last ounce of his pain and betrayal. Surprisingly, Sebastian's eyes were just as pained.

He ran his hand through his bloody, blond hair and held out his hand. "Let me see your arm, Jesse."

Without waiting for permission, Sebastian cradled Jesse's forearm in one hand and rolled up the sleeve of his red sweatshirt with the other. The warm, honey-colored skin of his arm was covered in shallow gashes, blood trickling from the wounds.

"I have a first-aid kit in the car. Maybe we should just ride over. It'll be faster."

Jesse was startled out of his daze at those words. This man, who just taken a spill that would have shaken a seasoned veteran, had just calmly suggested that they ride back. As if he hadn't just rocked Jesse's world down to its foundations with his revelation.

"Okay," he nodded. Fuck it. "You first."

THEY ENDED up at Jesse's place.

Sebastian had loaded the mountain bike into his car while Jesse had led the way on his new bike. His apartment was only seven blocks away from the park. They took the bikes inside the elevator and up to the eighth floor apartment.

"Come on in, Seb…" Jesse's voice trailed off, suddenly not knowing what to call the man. "Just park in the living room."

They cleaned up as best as they could. Jesse broke out the soap and water, peroxide and Band-Aids, and after much fussing over Sebastian and his bleeding scalp wound, Sebastian did take care of Jesse's arm.

Not that Jesse couldn't do it himself. But feeling Sebastian's soft fingers on his skin was an exhilarating treat. And he took such care, too. The way he gnawed on his lower lip as he cleaned out Jesse's wound with peroxide countered any discomfort Jesse was feeling at the time.

So tender.

Sebastian was way out of his league, though. So far out of out his league that Jesse didn't even bother asking him whether he swung his way at all.

Once Jesse's arm was covered with antibiotic ointment and appropriate adhesive bandages, he looked at the inexpert butterfly bandages that closed the gash over Sebastian's eyebrow, just where the foam of the helmet grabbed and ripped tender skin.

"Are you sure you don't want stitches?"

"I'll be fine," Sebastian waved it off as he washed his hands. "If I wind up with a scar, let it be a testament to having learned something new."

They ordered out for pizza, half without cheese, and Greek salad. Jesse brewed a pot of jasmine green tea while they waited.

"You'll definitely have a bruise. Even with ice it'll swell up a lot, and the road rash is already scabbing over," Jesse commented.

"I know. I can't go home like this." Sebastian paused, as if thinking, then pulled his phone out of his pocket, dialing a number.

"Renata, hello… no, I'm having dinner out…Yes, I'm with someone." Jesse watched Sebastian's long, slender fingers tap on the edge of the table with nervous impatience.

"No," he said, then paused. His eyebrows drew down into a frown, fine mouth tightening in what look like annoyance. "I said no. You'll have to host the family tomorrow with mom and dad… You're the one who invited them, Renata…. I have other business to attend to. In fact, I won't be back until after work Monday…"

Jesse watched as he pulled the phone away from his ear with a grimace; he could hear the tinny sound of his ex-girlfriend yelling through the speaker. Wincing, Sebastian brought it back to his ear. "Renata… Renata I will hang up if you don't stop shouting."

A long beat passed, her voice indistinct but still loud filtering through the receiver, and showing no signs of getting softer.

Sebastian hung up.

Their eyes met, wide gray and warm brown, and Jesse began to laugh.

"Oh my God, I should have learned to tell her off like that." Then his expression sobered.

"So… what should I call you, if you don't like 'Seb'?" he asked hesitantly.

The other man's lip quirked upwards in a faint smile before his expression smoothed. "Sebastian."

"Sebastian," the other repeated in a deep, sonorous voice. "I suppose you need a place to stay for the weekend, Sebastian."

"I can go to a hotel," he said. "I wouldn't want to impose, Jesse."

"Your company ain't an imposition," Jesse shrugged off Sebastian's objection. "Just, I want you to level with me."

Sebastian gave him his fully attention.

"Tell me why you didn't let me know who you were."

Sebastian leaned back in his chair, bringing his cup of tea to his mouth and taking a slow sip before setting it back down on the table between them.

"Well… this is a difficult situation," he began. "At first, I didn't realize our mutual connection to Renata. Once I knew – once I realized who you were—I didn't let you know, because…" He averted his eyes, drew in a deep breath, opened his mouth as if to answer, then took a second deep breath.

Lifting his gaze back to Jesse's face, he looked almost embarrassed. "I didn't tell you because I feared that once you knew me to be her 'pain-in-the-ass older brother', you'd no longer want to be my friend."

CHAPTER 4

JESSE AVOIDED direct eye contact. It would've been rude to scrutinize Sebastian during such a difficult moment. He'd been brought up to know that. What would his mother do for a guest going through a difficult time?

Offer him whiskey.

Hell no.

What would the Uncles do?

Jesse's mind turned to the older men on the rez. They sat in their rocking chairs on the porch, talking in hushed voices as they watched the young 'uns. When a guest showed up, he was invited in. Given a beer. Sometimes, he would stay for dinner. The basic rules of hospitality didn't change much from culture to culture and Jesse had adapted over the years.

But now, this. An emotional situation.

He had never witnessed his elders handle something like that – and by the time he was old enough to discern the nuances of what to expect and what to do, his mother was already deep in the bottle. His father had come back from Iraq about that time. Two weeks later, his dad took Jesse away.

His mother refused to go.

Life on a military base and a new school had thrust him into the world of Anglos, Blacks, and Hispanics with the occasional smattering of Asians. No other Natives, though – not that he could see. He adapted as best he could. He learned it was okay to look people in the eyes – most of the time anyway. People of Two Spirits had to pretend to like only the opposite sex, but the hospitality rules pretty much stayed the same.

Hospitality it was, then. Food was a comfort as well as a basic need. He'd feed Sebastian dinner.

Forty minutes later, the salad was all gone and the pizza was mostly demolished. Only one slice of the half-cheese-half-no-cheese pie remained in the cardboard box with its pepperoni and onions curled on top of the cold, waxy surface.

"You want the last piece?" Jesse asked.

"No… I'm no longer hungry. And it has cheese on it."

"Oh." Jesse considered Sebastian's response.

'I am no longer hungry.'

Did the slender man eat only when hungry? Was that part of his secret, part of why he had that sleek, strong, athletic body? Jesse fidgeted with his hands under the table. Had he been alone, he'd have devoured the last piece while standing over the sink and putting the rest of the dishes away. Yet he was comfortably full.

He really shouldn't.

Sighing deeply, he rose from the table and went to the sink, retrieving a roll of aluminum foil from one of the drawers beneath the counter. Returning to the table, he wrapped the single piece and put it in the freezer.

"You're saving that?" Sebastian asked, sounding intrigued.

"Yeah."

"You like pizza that much?"

"No…it's just pizza, but…wasting food is bad," he answered.

Jesse flinched as Kerrick slapped him again. "You don't work, you don't eat." He was Crow and he had his pride. There was no way he'd do the kind of work Kerrick demanded of him even though the pants were falling off his fifteen-year old hips. His ribs showed so much, he was embarrassed to change in front of others in his gym class. There was no money for food, let alone for soccer - not from Kerrick... but there was the 7-Eleven store and the cute clerk who would let him eat the sandwiches and donuts that would have to be thrown out at the end of her shift. She would wrap them in aluminum foil to disguise their contents from her shift manager; they were always waiting for him in a special bag under the counter.

Even if the sandwiches were only slices of soggy, pale bread holding a slice or two of reconstituted turkey lunchmeat and a limp leaf of lettuce, he was grateful for the meal, and always made sure to tell the clerk, a girl named Sue, 'thank you.'-

Wasting food wasn't just bad – for him, it meant starvation.

"JESSE? Are you alright?"

Sebastian's voice brought him back to the present.

He let go of the freezer handle and shook off the old memories. The feel of the foil in his hands, cool and familiar, along with Sebastian's question about saving a single slice of pizza had awakened the past, and he was eager to shove it back down where it belonged. Turning to face the other man, he plastered a smile on his face.

"Yeah," he answered, turning on the cheer, as false as it was. "So, if you get hungry, feel free to help yourself to anything in here, okay? And I mean anything. I'm gonna go hop in the shower real quick."

Without waiting for an answer, he vacated the kitchen as quickly as he could, hoping it didn't look like he was fleeing.

SEBASTIAN walked from the small kitchen through the tiny dining room, only to see Jesse disappear into his bedroom, and shortly after he heard the sound of the water running. His unexpected solitude gave him a welcome opportunity to look around. The apartment was smaller than his suite at the Gillen mansion, but it contained a lot more... stuff. The living room to his left seemed tidy on the surface, but duplicate items were almost everywhere. Sebastian spied a second television, an old CRT model, hiding behind the modern, thin one that sat on an old, particle-board entertainment center.

Three DVD players, seven speakers, two large boxes of various bits of electronic equipment, three keyboards, four computers; the electronic junk was piled into a tidy pyramid, occupying the corner between the sofa and the wall. The walls were covered with strip shelving and the shelves were crammed full of…well, a little bit everything, really. Sebastian wandered through the space in a clockwise scan, drinking everything in. An eclectic collection of books, some thicker tomes that turned out to be textbooks, stacks of well-thumbed paperbound manuals mixed in with jewel-cases containing computer disks both new and outdated, along with various bins filled…survival equipment?

There was a small hunting crossbow and its accompanying bolts, a variety of knives, a box of what appeared to be vegetable seeds, two extra boxes of table salt. Boxes of bicycle components and tools. Extra tubes of toothpaste and spare rolls of toilet paper.

Sebastian experienced an odd mixture of curiosity and concern. What did Jesse do with all this stuff? What was it for?

Was it really necessary to have three sleeping bags and two tents stuffed behind the sofa? Was it crucial to own hot pockets and Mylar thermal blankets and boxes of batteries for his numerous flashlights? Why was there a barely-used backpack, equipped with a solar panel, hanging by the door?

The shower was still running.

Curious as a cat about his sister's former boyfriend, he tiptoed back to the kitchen and opened the freezer. It was so full of small, aluminum-foil wrapped items, Sebastian was surprised that Jesse had been able to slide that extra piece of pizza in there. The cupboards contained a thrift store hodge-podge of plates and bowls and cups and glasses, four of each, none of them matching. The rest of the cabinets formed an extensive pantry of canned food. Soups, beans, chili, sauerkraut, tuna fish, and Spam were stacked alongside numerous boxes of pasta and bags upon bags of dried beans and rice. Had Jesse gotten stuck in his apartment for half a year, he'd never go hungry.

Sebastian cracked another door open to find sweets. Stale bags of old Halloween candy, junk cereals the store would almost give away for free, a few bars of chocolate. He lifted his eyebrows in surprise at the small jar of more expensive honey.

The floor creaked behind him, and Sebastian turned around to see Jesse in his bathrobe, wet hair toweled but not brushed out.

"What would you like, Sebastian?" he asked with a strange, eager expression. "I have some chocolate bars – or how about peanut butter cups?

"I don't really eat sweets," Sebastian murmured. "And anyway, I was just… exploring, I guess." His embarrassment at being caught snooping must have shown, he could feel warmth rise up his neck to his face. "Sorry. It's just… you've interesting things lying all over the place."

"Oh, right! No sweets!" It was as though Jesse had not only not minded the intrusion – he hadn't even recognized it as such. "I have some chips, or I can make some popcorn." Jesse surveyed the shelves packed with calories. "Pretty awesome, isn't it?"

THE BOY with a snake tattooed on the nape of his neck passed him a slice of bread and cheese on the way to their bedrooms. Feeding Jesse was punishable by corporal punishment, especially after the police had returned the escaped boy back to Kerrick for the second time, but Caleb had been given more than he needed to eat; he'd behaved and therefore had been suitably rewarded.

"I am a man of justice," Kerrick had said, his voice weighty with meaning. "You work, you eat."

And Caleb had worked almost every night. Some of his clients left him tips, which he kept hidden in a special place.

"We could get out of here together, Cal," Jesse said on the way to school, more than once. "We don't need him to survive."

And, eventually, they had. He'd learned a lot from his dad before he got deployed again. Now he was missing.

Dead, probably.

It would've been better had he let Jesse stay on the reservation, but the family was in turmoil, his mom was in rehab again, and when his dad had gone MIA half the world away, the nice neighbors he had been staying with had realized he would have to stay with them until the man returned—or didn't. Jesse could possibly be their responsibility for years.

Which is how he had ended up in the system.

They hitchhiked for weeks, chasing Jesse's dream of finding Crow ancestral lands in Ohio. But Ohio had been a wasteland of farms and rustbelt towns with no opportunities. They ended up in Pittsburgh, where the economy was on the upswing and where a trucker had told them they could find work off the books.

The light industrial warehouse they found on the South Side was a lot better than Kerrick's miserable excuse of a foster home. There wasn't much to steal but concrete construction block; therefore, the warehouse was left unguarded overnight. They could sneak in and out unobserved, and even better, they were able to use the bathroom and the shower behind the office.

Jesse had shared the expired sandwiches from Sue with equanimity, and they still made it to school and attended their classes, so their teachers were unaware of their situation.

Their way to school led through a square with a water fountain. They were able to fish for coins as long as the weather wasn't too cold. But the coins weren't enough for Caleb. Used to steady money from the clients Kerrick had sent his way, he didn't make as much cash on his own—and he'd grown used to the security the extra money represented. He'd disappear overnight only to show up in the morning with a fistful of money and those blood-shot, pinprick eyes.

"I DON'T actually need any snacks, but thank you, Jesse." Sebastian's melodious voice interrupted the ancient train of thought.

Yeah, it was bloody awesome to have enough food. And to share it, too. He looked at Sebastian, his lithe, lovely body settling on the sofa.

"You mentioned a movie, or is it getting too late?"

WHEN THE *Blood of Heroes* ended, midnight had already rolled by. Jesse suppressed a yawn. "If you go take your shower, I'll get the bedding ready in the meanwhile."

Sebastian nodded and departed through the bedroom and toward the bathroom in contemplative silence.

HE EMERGED from the bathroom with his hair wet and spikey from being toweled almost dry, and dressed in just his boxers. He was surprised to see one sleeping bag rolled out on the floor on top of another.

"Why not put it on the sofa, Jesse?"

"I'm too tall for the sofa."

"But I'm sleeping out here."

"No. Guests get the bed. It's a rule. Besides, I'm used to taking the floor from when Renata'd sleep over sometimes. You know, former girlfriend…" Jesse's voice drifted off.

They bickered for a while before Sebastian allowed Jesse to usher him into the small bedroom. The full-size bed was stuck against the wall, a stark testament to Jesse's lack of company. There were two chests of drawers and a closet full clothing and spare electronic equipment.

"I see," Sebastian said, when he opened it in order to hang his pants. "You could open a shop someday."

"I could. I used to work for a computer repair place, and the owner, Joe, he'd let me keep all these parts. They're still good." Jesse slid the closet door shut, revealing a floor-length mirror on one of the hollow-core panels.

"I think you'll be comfortable."

HE MUST have turned and tossed for several hours, unable to sleep. The bed was comfortable enough, but Sebastian's thoughts were on the big guy who was sleeping out on the living room floor.

As though sleeping on the floor was nothing out of the ordinary.

The heat kicked in again and Sebastian tossed the blanket away, touching one foot and a hand against the cooler wall. Every time he closed his eyes and relaxed, his limbs retracted and he woke up, feeling too warm again. He wedged his foot and hand between the mattress and the wall, closed his eyes, and relaxed experimentally.

Better.

Almost content, he wiggled a bit.

His hand brushed against something scratchy and dry – something that had no place behind the mattress. His fingers dug in without thinking. There was more. There was a lot more, whatever it was. He fished around, feeling a thin, rectangular package wedged between the mattress and the cool wall. He pulled it out and clicked on Jesse's reading light.

He was looking at a yogurt-coated cookie-dough Zone bar.

Incredulous, Sebastian fished out another packet, then another. Soon, the bed he was supposed to be sleeping on was covered with a sizable pile of various brands and flavors of nutrition and athletic bars. He was familiar with them; they were an athlete's junk food, a candy bar substitute, a quick energy fix on those days when one had no time to step out for lunch.

But so many?

And…who keeps food behind the bed?

Unable to sleep, Sebastian slid off the mattress. He dug his feet into the loopy brown carpet as he pulled the bed away from the wall.

Countless energy bars hissed as they spilled onto the soft floor. Sebastian sighed, lips pressed into a prim line, and started picking them up.

When he was done, what appeared to be Jesse's emergency food stash sat on the bed – a pile so large, he couldn't have slept there even had he wanted. Uncertain about what to do, he left it all there, grabbed the pillow and the blanket, and tiptoed his way into the living room. The old, brick-red sofa wasn't too short for him if he curled up a little bit. He soon fell asleep, lulled by the sound of Jesse's regular breathing.

THE SENSATION of fuzzy carpet rubbing against his knee woke Jesse the next morning. His eyes cracked open, and he smiled. He hadn't slept on the floor in ages. It wasn't as bad as he remembered it being, but then again he wasn't sleeping in a concrete warehouse anymore.

Turning on his back, he stretched his hands and feet as far away from one another as they'd go, making his limbs feel awake and alive. There was only a slight tinge from the injury on his left arm; the bandage covering the puncture wounds were still clean.

Jesse's eyes were suddenly arrested by the sight of Sebastian Gillen, whose lithe body was sprawled all over his sofa.

Why?

Jesse contemplated the possible reasons. He might have felt lonely, or maybe he didn't want Jesse to be the only one camping out, or he…no. Sebastian wouldn't seek out his company on account of a bad dream. He was stronger than that.

Jesse woke to thin arms hugging him from behind. It had gotten too cold for Caleb to find a trick willing to use an alley, and money was scarce. So was food. Caleb couldn't banish his demons with a needle anymore; nightmares drove him into Jesse's arms. He'd pull him in, run his fingers through Caleb's sweaty, spiky hair, offering what little comfort he could.

It was the least he could do for his best friend.

He tried to whisper his nightmares away.

Jesse gave a harsh swallow and turned on his side to face his guest. His hair was short like Caleb's had been. A fleeting curiosity stirred in Jesse's heart, wondering whether Sebastian's hair would also feel a bit rough and sweaty. He hoped not.

There was an unsettling sense of fragility, of delicacy, about Sebastian in his repose. Sleep softened his even features and gave his narrow lips the slightest hint of a smile. His long eyelashes were clearly delineated against the pale skin under his eyes. His smooth chest rose up and down with every breath, and Jesse saw the relaxed muscles that worked so hard to propel Sebastian through water almost every day.

He was stunning, gorgeous, like some precious fragile thing to be treasured and protected. An old emotion stirred in Jesse's heart.

He stomped on it, hard.

Sebastian wasn't like him. Sebastian probably had a girlfriend. He was heir to an ice cream empire, and there was an ice cream princess waiting in his future.

Sebastian wasn't one of Jesse's people. He didn't know what it was like, riding a horse bareback across the grassy plains and rugged mountains of the reservation. He had no idea what it was like to have your grandmother nod in approval as you held hands with another boy like it was a regular thing.

Which it was.

For Crow, and for most tribes that managed to rescue their traditions and mitigate the negative effect of missionaries, still had those that followed the old ways. Jesse would've been cherished and protected if the winds of fate hadn't torn him away from the mountains and the plains so long ago. He hadn't gone back.

He considered Sebastian again.

It wasn't anything Jesse hadn't seen before, but unlike in the pool, now he had the luxury of observing the handsome, even lovely, man in private.

So perfect.

He let his appreciative gaze travel down to where the rumpled blanket revealed a knobby knee, strong ligaments almost visible under the relaxed skin. The calf was deceptively smooth. Jesse knew how powerful those muscles must be to deliver the performance Sebastian required of them.

Has he no body hair at all?

Smooth, like a girl. Jesse was struck with the sudden desire to reach out and touch that silky, supple body to see what it felt like, discover if it really was as smooth and soft as it appeared.

SEBASTIAN'S eyes didn't quite open as he observed his new and only friend through a narrow crack in his eyelids. He feigned sleep to avoid the awkwardness which was sure to follow if Jesse realized he had been awake and aware of his scrutiny. As Jesse's heavy gaze traveled down his form, he slid his covert gaze up to broad shoulders and strong arms. Jesse was wearing a t-shirt, so the interesting tattoos on his back and arm weren't currently on display, but Sebastian remembered every line, every angle and twist of the sinuous design. They seemed vaguely exotic—tribal even.

Jesse unzipped his sleeping bag and slowly stood up, his boxer shorts revealing long legs, their skin unmarred by ink.

His hamstrings are getting defined. I hope he's been stretching.

There was powerful muscle mass hiding underneath Jesse's lightly insulated skin, and Sebastian wished for more boldness and courage – the kind that would have allowed him to reach out and touch Jesse's thigh, feeling the well-shaped quadriceps which was so close to being revealed to the naked eye.

Careful to avoid being detected, Sebastian allowed his gaze to travel further up Jesse's strong form, pausing on the round curve of his ass, then moving higher, to the waist above it, still a bit large in girth, and the love handles right above Jesse's pelvic bone. Yet, the beer belly was slowly diminishing and the handsome face, even though still boyishly soft, showed promise of a strong jaw and prominent cheekbones.

Beautiful. He's just...*beautiful.*

The realization made Sebastian's face warm with a slight flush. He watched Jesse roll up his sleeping bags and shove them to the side. The man wasn't even his type. He liked softer, more feminine men. Shorter men. Less muscled men. His mind flitted to his hair stylist. Now there was a man he'd like to date, except the stormy-eyed, lithe beauty had long been taken by his bald-headed masseuse partner.

His sudden… attraction… to a guy he met at the pool, minor as it was, made no sense.

He sighed.

The sound, unfortunately, attracted the other man's attention.

"SEBASTIAN! Hey… good morning. Sorry I woke you." Jesse's troubled brow smoothed as he smiled at his guest. "So what happened? Can't sleep alone?" The words flew out of his mouth unchecked, as they often did, and he was appalled to see the prone man sit up with a slight blush on his face.

"I'm very sorry, Jesse…I don't quite know it happened, but, um… I made a mess on your bed."

"Oh." Jesse looked away. No wonder the poor man was embarrassed. "Well, you know where to find the shower. How 'bout you rinse off and freshen up and I'll take care of the sheets." His kind, warm brown eyes held a lively sparkle entirely free of ridicule as he met Sebastian's panicked expression. He raised his right hand in the air, palm out.

"No. Don't say anything. It could've happened to anyone. We aren't masters of our bodies while asleep. Please… no apologies."

His formerly fastidious, funny, intelligent partner in survival was looking thinner and thinner, the tracks that marred his supple arms hidden under several layers of old, worn-out shirts the charity shelter had to spare. His formerly bright, eucalyptus-green eyes were occluded with a smoky haze now, and blood-shot; their pupils narrow. Caleb no longer knew what he was doing during such times and, occasionally, he'd wake up wet and smelly like a four-year old. Then it fell to Jesse to help him find clean clothes from his plastic bag and usher his thin, trembling body into the shower.

Not even the cheapest johns wanted him anymore.

Then, one freezing day, Caleb just disappeared.

Jesse figured these things just happened. He walked into his bedroom, chin high and proud, determined not to give his guest a single reason for embarrassment or shame.

He stopped in his tracks.

His…his stash.

Revealed.

Guilt and shame suffused him. He knew stashing food behind his bed just wasn't done – Renata had made that painfully clear - but it had made him sleep so much better, just knowing it was there, within arm's reach, non-perishable. He knew it was peculiar, but it a safety blanket he wasn't willing to give up just yet.

Hunger pangs struck him just then and there.

He felt exposed and deprived and humiliated and, sliding into his cast-off sweats and a hoodie, he shoved a few assorted nutrition bars into his pockets, slipped his Nike's onto his bare feet. He snuck out the door.

SEBASTIAN had no urgent need to wash up. Instead, he observed his host's startled reaction at the exposition of his treasure hoard. He'd seen the warring emotions in his face, the rising red tide coming up to meet the hairline of jet-black hair. There was despair and sadness and fear in his eyes, and that scary far-away look, during which the former warmth had no longer been in evidence.

He watched as Jesse dressed in haste, stuffed his pockets with all they could hold, and left, all without giving him a second look.

Oh God. What have I done?

Sebastian threw his clothes on just as fast and ran out of the apartment and down the stories of the emergency exit staircase. The pounding of his feet echoed in the concrete stairwell, graffiti flashed by, and he felt dizzy from turning to the left after every flight. His thighs began to burn as he controlled his rapid descent, determined to beat the elevator and catch Jesse in the lobby.

He burst into the modest foyer only to hear the elevator door ding closed. A wash of fresh, cool air met his face and neck, cold creeping under his shirt as the glass door to the street slowly drifted shut.

Sebastian burst through it on the run and looked up and down the paved sidewalk. The tall, concrete apartment buildings were nestled close together and the streets around them were crowded with parked cars. The easy Saturday traffic from a nearby highway was but a light sound screen in the background of his mind as he whirled, peering up and down the street in search of Jesse's familiar figure.

Black.

Black hair, black hoodie.

There.

He saw him turn the corner of the behemoth complex. His legs burst into a run on their own accord. Dodging pedestrians, he was determined to follow.

CHAPTER 5

BEFORE Sebastian gave chase, he ground to a stop and bent over to tie his shoes. Then he burst into a run, weaving amongst the placid pedestrians. Guys were out with basketballs and dogs and children. Women pushed strollers, and the occasional couple carried groceries from a car parked far away. He felt very white in this neighborhood, blond, and conspicuous. His elbow jostled a big guy with a shaved head that gleamed like burnished wood.

"Watch it, asshole!"

"Sorry..." he breathed out, but with little attention. He quickened his pace.

Focused on catching up to Jesse, he turned the corner only to see him cross the street, walking at a brisk pace.

Two blocks later Sebastian almost caught up with his target and slowed to a fast walk, gasping for air. He was in shape for long-distance swimming, not short-distance sprinting. It had been years since he had done any serious running, and his physical condition both surprised and appalled him.

I used to run five miles a day just to cross-train.

Jesse didn't seem to have noticed him and Sebastian wasn't sure, exactly, what to do. Talking about embarrassing subjects wasn't his strong suit. If anything, he avoided awkward conversations at all costs. Had Renata been here she would have known exactly what to say. She would have, quite certainly, been able to shed light on Jesse's behavior, should Sebastian choose to ask her, but asking her would reopen old wounds for both his sister and his friend. Asking questions about personal matters had never been remotely near his comfort zone. For now, however, all he could do was follow.

A SLIGHT flicker of gold and white in his peripheral vision had caught Jesse's attention four blocks ago. He forged on, heedless of the man following him.

Oh God.

Oh god oh god oh god.

He'll figure I'm some deranged nut.

Fragments of old arguments floated into his mind. Renata, her shoulder-length, auburn hair wisping around her petite face, blue eyes disapproving. Shrill voice barking commands, telling him what to do and what not to do if he wanted to be acceptable to her brother and be allowed to stay by her side.

He had been unable to tell her why he'd been doing all those things.

He knew why, though.

Fully aware of his fears, he knew where his quirks had come from but that didn't mean he wanted to talk about them, nor were they all that simple to change. Renata was a pampered, sheltered society girl, and there were things one just didn't share with pampered, sheltered society girls:

"I keep all those protein-bars right next to me because fainting from hunger is always humiliating, embarrassing, and potentially dangerous, Renata."

"I can't let you get closer because you try to control me and a bad man once tried to control me in the past, Renata."

"Next time I'm homeless, at least I'll have all I need to camp out and live off the land because I'll never let a man bend me over for a piece of bread like Caleb did, Renata.."

Yeah, that would've gone over well. Renata would've thought he was a nutcase just because he needed to plan ahead. It wasn't like it was a bad thing, right? He just needed to know he had all his bases covered, especially now, with the threat of the triathlon looming only five months ahead.

If he failed to perform, old man Easton would fire his ass. Getting fired would mean no money, and no money would mean no food. No amount of spare change fished out of water fountains would help him cover his expenses, either. Even going back to Joe and doing computer repair would be an uncertain proposition. The man was as cheap as employers went and he did nothing without an ulterior motive.

Nobody would ever call him a 'mooch' again.

JESSE CROSSED the street, entering the park where he had met Sebastian the day before. The man had caught up to him, following maybe three steps behind.

He broke into an easy jog. The asphalt path rose to meet him and he embraced the impact he felt when the balls of his feet hit its surface.

One-two-three-four,
One-two-three.
One-two-three-four,
One-two-three.

His breathing steadied into a pattern he'd read about and tried to practice, inhaling for four steps and exhaling for three. The pleasant, late February day warmed up to mid-forties and would've been ideal for running, had it not been for the sound of sneakers hitting the pavement right behind him.

Jesse sped up.

He didn't want to talk.

One-two-three,
One-two.

One-two-three,

One-two.

He had to make fewer footfalls per breath now. Running faster was more work. Blood sang in his veins, his body warming up and responding to his desire for more.

He passed the swan pond. The waterspout wasn't turned on and the swans hadn't yet returned, the season being still too cold. That's where he usually took his first break, but the persistent slap of footfalls dogged his heels. Stopping didn't even cross his mind.

SEBASTIAN disciplined himself to breathe as he used to know how, matching Jesse step for step. They fell into a rhythm now, jogging almost side by side in an awkward silence. It occurred to Sebastian how odd it seemed, to be running a step behind his interesting friend.

Friend.

There was that coveted word again. His friend was in pain and Sebastian wanted to help, to be of comfort, yet acknowledging such pain would only make it worse. He focused on just being there, and being there meant running instead of stopping and doubling over, which was what he really wanted to do just then.

If Jesse could push through, so could he.

Relief washed over him as Jesse slowed to a walk. Breath tore in and out of him, fast and painful and furious, drawing in air, struggling for gas exchange.

He did the same. The last bits of his extra energy were spent on pulling up so that he and Jesse now walked side by side, their pace moderate as they caught their breath.

Sebastian saw the tempting hand next to him and had to stop himself from reaching out. There was nothing he wanted more at that moment than to brush those fingers with his own, yet his own sense of awkward restraint stopped him again.

His usual calm reserve – how he loathed it. Momentary wishes acted upon, those human impulses that made the world work for the rest of humanity, were forbidden fruit to him. It was his ultimate armor against the world – it kept others out. It was also his prison.

"You cannot!" His father's resounding voice filled his mind. The ice cream magnate looked at his heir in bewilderment. "Others may go train for the Olympics, but you're a senior at Yale. You're a Gillen. A Gillen does not yield to the pursuit of vainglory. A Gillen goes to Wharton and learns about the business he will soon inherit."

Sebastian felt his sinuses fill with no warning whatsoever, liquid flooding all the way up to his eyes. He'd been so fast – the qualifiers pointed to him as a logical candidate. He could have been a contender.

Yet, a Gillen did not shed tears.

A Gillen did not let others in.

Being a Gillen was an unasked-for burden that he'd resented ever since the wings of his dreams had been clipped, locking him into a gilded cage so that he would sell a product he loathed.

For the rest of his life he'd peddle the cold, sweet confection during the day.

When night fell, he'd go swimming. While his strong arms cut through the soothing water with a smooth and silent stroke, he'd dream of what could have been.

He carded his fingers through his hair and swept droplets of sweat out of his eyes. In years past, the sweat would have been accompanied by tears at the memories. Now, he just focused on controlling his breathing. He'd learned to suppress everything else for the sake of duty, dignity, and familial harmony.

JESSE CHANCED a glance to his left. Sebastian walked next to him, sweaty, breathing hard as he himself struggled for breath. It surprised him. Sebastian Gillen was a great swimmer, yet his conditioning didn't translate to dry land. On it, they were equals.

Equally inept.

The thought humored him enough that he tossed a grin at Sebastian. His friend, one who had followed him when he'd run out of his apartment in distress, the one who had kept him silent company, not prying, not beseeching him to stop and change and be something he wasn't.

Sebastian looked at him with those calm, serious eyes. So gray…they were warm, like the folds of the gray woolen blanket he had used to huddle under all those years ago.

They stopped, their gazes locked.

"How far do you usually run?" Sebastian asked. Jesse knew that wasn't the question burning in his mind and gave him a solemn look, once again appreciating Sebastian's restraint.

"I still do the walk-run thing. I go across the park and back, three times a week." He gave Sebastian a sheepish smile. "This was the first time I actually ran a mile."

"This has been the first time I've run a mile in many years," Sebastian said and Jesse could have sworn that his voice had just a tinge of a bitter edge to it. His eyes returned to the other, quickly enough to discern a crack in the calm façade that showed a world of pain underneath.

The man has everything. What would he be in pain about?

Jesse caught his thought and rolled it around in his mind. It felt somewhat unworthy and shallow to assume that a man who had wealth and a position of authority felt no pain, and he felt an unexpected pang of embarrassment for thinking otherwise.

"It's easier to run a mile when you do it with a friend," he said with casual ease, allowing a slow, charismatic grin to light up his features.

THERE IT was again. They resumed walking and Jesse had said that magic word.

"…with a friend…"

Something threatened to snap within Sebastian. The feeling frightened him. He hadn't felt that way since, since…

"*I don't need your money, Father. I've had offers from corpo-rate sponsors to take me through my training.*"

"*Have you?*" *Johan Gillen raised his prominent eyebrows.* "*How long do you think that will last?*"

The threat in his voice was unmistakable. His business connections, his club – they would respect his wishes more than his son had done. They'd cooperate.

"*I can always work.*"

"*You can perform a job of little significance, being paid barely enough to live on. Not much will come of that.*"

Sebastian wished he'd taken Steve White, his old college room-mate, up on his offer to work for his family's candy company. He could have gotten out of the house, the pay would have been de-cent compared to other fresh-out-of-college options, and Steve and his family would have supported his decision to train for the Olympics. Yet hesitation cost him his opportunity. Steve had been a friend. Where was he now?

Sebastian broke into an easy jog. Now it was he who was chased by the demons of his past. Jesse fell in step right next to him.

"Let's do your walk-run. You lead," Sebastian gasped between breaths.

"Okay."

Half an hour later, Jesse announced their last burst of speed and they finished on the other side of the park, sweaty and dying of thirst.

"I usually carry water," Jesse said, apologetic.

"I have a wallet on me. How about we stretch out – then we can go get some breakfast?"

Jesse hesitated.

"You do need to stretch. Your hamstrings are getting more defined."

The simple observation lit Jesse's face with a smile and a flush even deeper than his workout glow. "Really?"

"Yes." Sebastian nodded. "I never see you stretch at the pool and that's asking for an injury, Jesse. Here. This grass is only a little wet…"

FIVE MINUTES later, Jesse was in pain. No stretch should've made him feel like this. He ended up lying on his back, Sebastian's one hand pushing his right knee down and the other holding his heel in the air. His toes pointed over his chest and his hamstrings burned like an over-tuned guitar.

"Tighten your muscles and press against my palm." The calm command had Jesse pushing his heel into Sebastian's unwavering hand.

"Now bend the knee a little and relax." Jesse did so, only to have Sebastian move the stubborn limb further up.

"Ahh…ow."

He felt Sebastian ease off a bit. "It's not supposed to hurt too much. Just a bit of discomfort, but not real pain."

Amazing. The leg inched its way up and over Jesse's chest. This was the last of it and he'd be allowed to lower his limb, just like he'd done with the other one. And just like with his first leg, Sebastian ran his fingers up and down the back of his tight hamstrings, his fingers seeking out knots and dissolving them with a few well-placed, skilled touches.

"Where did you learn how to do this?"

"Yolanda."

Jesse sank into the familiar sensations of admiration and lust. The other man had small hands, but they were a lot stronger than they looked.

Like the rest of him.

… so fucking gorgeous…

The thought hit him like a sledgehammer. Jesse stopped right then and there. Sebastian was a friend. Probably straight. Jesse resolved to do his best and not act on his fervent desire to run his hands over Sebastian's smooth skin, to take Sebastian's composed lips in his own and kiss him until he melted in his arms.

No, thinking like that would lead nowhere good.

And now he had a boner to hide under his sweats.

TWENTY MINUTES later, Jesse was staring at a menu. Prior to the commencement of his triathlon training, he would have had two Hostess fruit pies and a cup of coffee. They were cheap, only two for a dollar, and they packed a real punch of happy, sugary fruitiness. About a week into his training, he found they no longer tasted all that great and he upgraded to inexpensive egg-and-biscuit sandwiches from a local fast-food joint. They gave him enough fuel to keep going all the way till lunch – especially when he used the "Buy-two-get-one-free" coupons. Using the coupons made him less guilty about spending two dollars instead of one.

About six weeks into his training he had met Sebastian, and by the end of February, his tastes had shifted away from cheap fast-food to making his own scrambled eggs at home. He loved eggs. They packed a punch of energy and protein and vitamins, and if he had two slices of whole-wheat toast along with them, they didn't make him feel bloated like the fast-food sandwiches used to.

Now he was seated across from Sebastian, the slender and muscular super-swimmer and businessman extraordinaire, and he couldn't decide what to eat. Normally he'd just have his three eggs and two slices of toast, but the bistro had blueberry pancakes on the menu. He ran his tongue along the sharp edges of his teeth. Biting into a soft pancake, bursting the warm blueberry within and feeling the juices dissolve on your tongue – that would've been just so, so...

"Happy Birthday, Jesse!" He lifted his ten-year old eyes to his foster-grandmother and grinned. He knew. She knew he knew, and he knew she knew he knew that his very favorite breakfast were blueberry pancakes. It was hardly a surprise when she lifted a large, domed lid off of a pan waiting in the warm oven, displaying a batch of blue-dotted pancakes she'd made before he woke up.

"Aww, Granny… you're the best!" He flashed her his brightest, happiest grin. His mother had gone to rehab when he was twelve, and his dad took took him off the reservation a year before his reserve unit got activated. Jesse had e-mailed with him weekly until one day the scheduled letter failed to arrive. That was two years ago. He hadn't heard from him since. His last foster home had sucked, but this lady seemed… nice. Real nice. He caught the glimmer in her warm eyes, and as he tasted his most-favoritest-bestest-ever breakfast, he felt loved for the first time in two years.

"JESSE." Even though his voice was calm, Sebastian's tone held soft reproach. "Are you ready to order yet?"

He sighed. "Well… there's what I should eat, and there's what I really want to eat."

Wide, gray eyes met frustrated brown. "Proceed."

"Hmm… I should eat eggs and whole-wheat toast, but what I really want is blueberry pancakes. Except I can't have those because they are not 'triathlon food'. And if I blow the triathlon, I'll get fired, and if I get fired…" Jesse trailed off, having said too much by far. His nose made a hissing sound as he drew a deep breath and produced an even deeper exhale.

"I'm sorry, Sebastian. I…I don't mean to be such trouble."

Sebastian lifted his fine, thin eyebrows and his gray eyes sparkled with interest. "You are no trouble to me. Ahh… how about you have both?"

"Both eggs and blueberry pancakes?" Jesse's eyes widened.

"Yes. Both eggs and blueberry pancakes."

Jesse glanced at the menu again. Eight dollars for the pancakes, four for the eggs and toast, two for his large coffee. Fourteen dollars for one breakfast plus tip. Nowadays he'd only spend that much on his breakfast for the whole week.

"No—no, that's too much."

And somehow, Sebastian knew. He didn't know how the other man knew that his 'too much' referred to money instead of the amount of food, but he had already noticed that Sebastian didn't miss much. The businessman was quietly observant, and intuitive—qualities that were necessary in running a vast ice cream empire, but uncomfortable when they were directed at him.

The waitress appeared again, harried and impatient. "Have you two decided yet?"

"Yes," Sebastian answered, before Jesse could object further. "We'll both have the blueberry pancakes and the scrambled eggs with a side of whole wheat toast. No butter on the toast and only real butter on the pancakes. I'll have tea; he'll have coffee. And extra water for both of us, please."

"Sure." She sauntered off, carried by the ebb and flow of her work.

The awkward silence she left behind stretched and strained.

"Thank you for letting me stay for the weekend, Jesse," Sebastian said, breaking the silence between them finally. "The least I can do is treat you to breakfast…. Please, let me do this."

AND SO it came to pass that Jesse Hightower had both his triathlon-approved eggs and his heart's desire, blueberry pancakes. His appetite wasn't nearly large enough to eat everything after his run, however, and after two glasses of water, one cup of coffee with cream, half the eggs and half the pancakes, he was well and thoroughly full.

And so was Sebastian. Jesse watched the man place the fork and knife parallel to each other on the plate, signaling the end of his repast. He looked at his own plate. He felt comfortable and warm and still had the taste of blueberries and syrup in his mouth. He wanted to experience that heart-warming sensation again and again, but his stomach protested and he knew, without having to be told, that if he finished all the food, the walk back home would be a miserable experience indeed.

"This was so good," he said finally.

"It was. I'm glad you enjoyed it." Sebastian's mouth curved upward into a pleased smile. Jesse eyed the leftover food, afraid he looked like a smitten ten-year old–and that was funny alright–but inside he was waged in a dark and serious. Across from him, Sebastian sat utterly still, as though he didn't dare interfere.

As though he knew what Jesse was fighting.

"I just don't want it to go to waste," he said, after long moments. Sebastian nodded, still silent.

"It would be so…" He stilled his tongue, realizing that he was giving too much away. He tried to school his face into something more neutral, not sure if he succeeded.

The arrival of their waitress was a welcome interruption. "Still working at it?"

"I will have mine to go," Sebastian said, and she nodded, not seeming to mind the imperious note in his voice. She nodded, turning and walking away, but was back in a moment or two, handing him an aluminum pie tin with a lid.

"Anything else?" she asked, her tone bored.

Sebastian paid her little attention, busy sliding half of the remains of his generous brunch into the pie tin. He glanced up at Jesse from under long eyelashes. "I find leftovers taste best the next day," he remarked, an obvious hint, but Jesse was still uncertain.

It felt like forever before Jesse gave into temptation, and he turned to the waitress, who managed to look polite and bored and a touch impatient all at the same time. "Can I… can I have one of these containers too, please?"

The waitress rolled her eyes and sighed and stalked away, leaving Jesse with a blush creeping up his face.

A middle-aged couple approached their car. The man unlocked it while the woman held their take-out containers. Their lunch was over and they were ready to head back to the office. Jesse approached the man as he was about to close the door, a spray-bottle of window-cleaner in one hand and a wad of paper-towels in the other. He started to spray and wipe the windshield, hoping for a tip.

"Hey, kid, whatcha think you're doing?" He was irate and territorial, not caring for the unspoken obligation the unasked-for service carried.

"Just bein' nice," Jesse grinned.

"You need your drug money that bad?" The man in the suit sneered. Jesse stopped, his face white as a sheet. Only last week he had come back to find Caleb cold and stiff in their corner of their warehouse, rubber tourniquet still around his arm and the needle still in his arm.

"No. No! I never! I..." Tears hovered at the rims of his eyes as he grasped the bottle harder, squirting and squirting, wasting the precious blue liquid against the cold, smooth glass. The paper towel in his other hand was soaked, coming apart as he ground it into the spotless windshield.

The occasional car passed them.

"Hey kid..." The man got out of the car and grabbed his arm. "You can stop now. I just don't wanna support anyone's habit, is all."

Then the woman stepped back out of the car in her smart business suit, her heels clicking as she circled around the hood toward Jesse.

"Here. If you want food, take these." She handed him the plastic bag with two still-warm aluminum pie tins, both covered and sealed. Her voice held as much pity as the man's voice had dripped with scorn.

"Thank you," Jesse let out with a shaky breath, unable to meet her eyes with his wet ones. "Thank you very much, ma'am. You are very kind." He stood there, a spray bottle and a wad of soaked paper towel in one hand and the warm, fragrant package in the other, unable to move. By the time he was ready to look up again, the car was gone.

Sebastian was sitting right across the table from him, sipping what was left of his water. He appeared immovable, like a giant rock, sheltering him from the raging current that was their waitress's impatience. Jesse's take-out container sat before him, waiting.

Slowly, Jesse blinked and released the breath he'd been holding. Then slid the remainder of his pancakes, toast, and eggs into the container, putting the lid in place and sealing it with care.

"Here—don't forget your syrup." Sebastian handed Jesse two

unopened tubs of the thick, maple-flavored liquid that had been provided with their pancakes.

"Thank you." He couldn't look at the other man, keeping his gaze focused on placing the syrup in the container.

"Jesse," Sebastian said, and something in the blond's voice made Jesse look up, through damp eyelashes. "That woman was insufferable. She will not be tipped."

Jesse forced a smile. "Not her fault. It's... it's mine." The waitress most likely had her own cross to bear.

"Decent manners aren't optional. Not when people deal with you, Jesse. You're worth a lot more than you realize."

Sebastian's words echoed in Jesse's mind as he navigated his way between the busy tables, following in Sebastian's wake. Something heavy and tight began to loosen within him as he searched his mind for the last time anyone had addressed him in words this kind.

THEY WALKED back to Jesse's apartment in companionable silence. Their takeout containers were no longer warm in their hands when they reached Jesse's side of the park, and instead of hard concrete, the wakening earth was soft under their feet. The sun was out, and a few of the birds had already returned from their winter migration, chirping in the bare branches of the stately sycamores overhead. Recent rains and warmer temperatures had greened the chartreuse grass; purple and yellow crocuses shone like jewels by their feet.

Jesse noticed none of this. His thoughts were on the takeout container in Sebastian's hands.

Would the rich man actually eat microwaved leftovers the next day?

This was Renata's uppity, pain-in-the-ass brother.

Except he was so nice.

Was it common for him not to finish what he ordered and paid for?

Had Jesse not been there, would he have just left the food, allowing it to be discarded like so much garbage?

Would he have eaten something fancier instead?

"Jesse."

"Yes?" He glanced over, pulled from his thoughts.

"I have decided to enter the triathlon as well."

Jesse stopped in his tracks.

"What?"

"I don't like to repeat myself, Jesse, but for you, I'll say it as many times as you need to hear it." Sebastian's tone was at odds with his smile.

"I just have a hard time believing what you just said, Sebastian."

Sebastian lifted his shoulders, still clad in his old Yale shirt from yesterday, and dropped them in an eloquent shrug.

"I have… regrets. Regrets about an opportunity in life I allowed to slip by, many years ago. Maybe doing the triathlon with you will give me my opportunity back."

The gray eyes slid down and away, his expression veiled from Jesse's searching gaze.

"The training is time-consuming, Sebastian. It's hard."

Sebastian turned away, ready to emerge from under the crowns of the trees and back onto the sidewalk. As Jesse jogged to catch up with him, he thought he heard him say something in a quiet, almost shy voice. He strained to hear over the sounds of car traffic nearby, not willing to let Sebastian's words be carried away with the wind. "Say again?"

Sebastian glanced at him, his bossy certainty a thing of the past. "It's always easier with a friend."

CHAPTER 6

HIS FACE still flushed and sweat dripping off his brow, Jesse burst through the doors of Eleventh Hour Security. Getting a run in was a good thing, but being late was highly discouraged. He swung by his cubicle and grabbed a backpack on the way to the restroom.

Running was logistically more demanding than swimming, in that he never came back from the pool smelly and dripping with sweat. Several days had passed since the disastrous bike lesson in the park, but Sebastian's cut was still too raw to brave the chlorinated water, and his own puncture wound was still scabbed over. They had decided to give swimming a rest for one week and run instead. Jesse didn't know how Sebastian managed to restore his appearance to his usual calm, professional self, but Jesse kept running into grooming difficulties.

He was sweaty all over.

According to the training sites he frequented, it was a good sign. His body had become accustomed to aerobic exercise and his cooling systems were now more efficient.

Sweat was sticky.

Inconvenient.

It didn't take long before it began to smell.

Jesse fished a small washcloth out of his backpack and wet it under cold water, wiping down as best he could. A somewhat larger towel followed, drying off the water and the still-emerging beads of perspiration. Then deodorant… then a clean shirt, dry underwear, dry socks. He'd never gone through so much laundry before.

Hurried brush strokes tamed his hair once again, and he tied it up in a ponytail at the nape of his neck, letting it hang down below his shoulder blades.

He was hot.

Hot and itchy.

There was no way in hell he'd get any work done with the wet, itchy heating pad of his hair resting against his neck. Resigned, he pulled out the bandanna that he used to hold back his hair during his runs with Sebastian. He shook it out, flattened it, folded it carefully, and tied his ponytail up and away from his steaming skin.

He sighed with relief as he felt cool air against his heated flesh. Glancing up at his reflection in the mirror hanging above the sink, he snorted. His damp hair had already begun to escape its confines, frizzing from the humidity that came off his skin. He thought of fussing with it, but his eyes fell on his watch.

Late again. Damn.

Jesse sauntered back to his cubicle, hoping nobody noticed his leisurely arrival.

THIRD consecutive run this week, and Sebastian was already stiff and sore. Swimming was so much easier, gentler, cooler. Especially now, with the early spring sun scorching his skin. He'd have to remember to start packing sunscreen. Yet, despite the itch of sweat and his sore feet, he was happy to be in the park, because he was there with Jesse.

Every cloud has a silver lining.

Sebastian exhaled through his mouth, counting his breaths like Jesse was doing beside him. They moved at a steady clip, passing under the still leafless trees, the increasing heat of sunshine kissing their skin.

Sebastian was happy.

Yes, happy.

For the first time in years, he ran without too much trouble. The periodic walk breaks were a strategic aid to allow both himself and Jesse to make the best out of their thirty-five-minute workout. That was all either could spare during their respective lunch breaks, as they both had to change both before and after, and appear halfway presentable once they were finished.

There had been a time when Sebastian could have run a five-kilometer race under thirty minutes, but he'd never felt so light and giddy as he did now.

It's easier with a friend.

Jesse's words made him smile. A real, uncensored, full-out smile that went up to his eyes and made the corners of his eyes crinkle. He didn't know whether it was Jesse's company or the workout itself, but he was buoyed by optimism. Sebastian knew that with time, and a little patience, they would both rung long and fast, and the minor inconveniences he was experiencing these past few days would go away.

Now he was running with a training partner. With a friend.

Even though the word no longer shocked him the way it had before, he still relished its shape in his mind, on his tongue.

On his tongue.

Had they not been running, Sebastian wouldn't have been able to excuse his flush as simple exertion. Jesse was tall, and broad, and handsome, with a winning smile and a go-getter attitude. He'd obviously been marked by something tragic in his past, yet he had still managed to retain a kind disposition and a cheerful outlook. Jesse fascinated him.

Sebastian had a sudden yearning to run his tongue up the tattoos twining up his arm and taste the sweat on Jesse's flushed skin. The sudden desire surprised him. Jesse was a friend. He'd dated Sebastian's sister, and was most likely straight. Muddying the waters with hot, heavy looks and inappropriate thoughts about the other man could ruin things completely, and Sebastian cherished their budding friendship too much to risk it falling apart because he found the other man attractive.

Think of work.

Think of ice cream.

Think of market surveys.

Jesse was a friend. A male friend, a straight friend. An off-limits, I-won't-screw-this-up friend.

"HEY, PRINCESS!" The bold, gravelly voice brought him to the present. He knew that voice all too well from Chamber of Commerce meetings. They rarely agreed on anything.

Every silver lining has a cloud.

Sebastian and Jesse slowed down as one to turn around and face the tall, imposing figure of Tyler Easton.

"Tyler," Sebastian nodded, breathing hard.

"Hey, boss," Jesse said. "What'cha doin' out?"

"Runnin'," Tyler grinned. "Just like you two wanna-be's." His sharp gaze was assessing as he studied them.

"How's the trainin', Hightower?" Tyler asked. "Can ya swim without drownin' yet?"

Jesse shrugged. He didn't want to give too much away, yet he didn't want to look like a computer-jockey wimp, either.

"It's okay," he allowed. "I'm workin' on my bilateral breathin' now." Saying that didn't volunteer how far he could or couldn't swim, nor how fast. Breathing on both sides was a slightly advanced technique, however, and Jesse was satisfied to see Tyler's eyebrows rise in surprise.

"See ya inside, Hightower. Good seein' ya, Princess." He nodded to Sebastian Gillen and turned around, jogging toward their office building in an easy, predatory lope.

Jesse slid a glance toward Sebastian. His breath stuttered at his grim expression. Jesse stopped, propped the palms of his hands on his knees, and sucked in few breaths of air. Sebastian, predictably, circled back to him and stopped as well.

"You okay, Jesse?"

Jesse straightened. They were almost done with their run and should be cooling down anyway. "You know him?"

"Tyler Easton? We've met."

Jesse noted the way Sebastian's jaw tightened and a muscle in his neck jumped. Self-restraint went only so far.

"He pisses you off," Jesse said, gleefully. "He calls you Princess and you don't like that much." He was fishing, hoping to find out more about both Sebastian and his boss. Getting dirt on Tyler Easton would be especially delicious. Jesse was already planning what sorts of pranks he and the boys could play around the office. Their hard-driving, cantankerous boss was generally a pain in the ass, but he could take a joke, and he had his employees' respect.

Sebastian shook his head. "Long story." He glanced at his watch. "Let's walk and stretch out. How are your abductors? Have you been stretching before bed?"

Jesse chose not to comment on the change of topic, and subjected himself to Sebastian's expert instruction.

"THE SERVERS are backed up on the secondary systems," Jesse reported, glancing at his notes. "The data goes from our client's site to the primary systems first and gets backed up at ten minute intervals… here," Jesse turned the page, showing the flow diagram of the newly-installed system to Tyler.

Half an hour of questions and answers later, Tyler leaned back with a satisfied smile.

"All right. Looks good. Proceed with testing, then."

"Sure, boss."

Jesse turned to leave when Tyler raised his voice again.

"So… you know Gillen?"

He turned to face Tyler again.

"Yeah."

"Where from?" Tyler's tone was neutral and Jesse didn't see any harm in answering his question.

"From the pool. I had some trouble with my swimming so he loaned me his coach. She's really great, you know. She helped me with my technique so much!"

"Oh yeah?" Tyler grinned. "And now you run together, too?"

"Not really," Jesse shrugged. "It's just until our wounds heal up."

"Wounds?" Tyler straightened to his full and impressive height, eyes wide and his expression betraying a great deal of curiosity.

"Well, from the biking accident… I figured, since Sebastian helped me with my swimming, I'd teach him how to ride a bike."

"He lets you call him Sebastian? That fucking, stuck-up, pseudo-European prick. Not many people get away with that. D'ya realize how long it took to even learn his first name?"

Jesse shrugged. His friend was a bit introverted, was all.

"So Gillen didn't know how to bike?" Tyler continued to satisfy his curiosity.

"N… no," Jesse shook his head, still amazed at the fact. "He prefers horses, but he was a quick study." Jesse paused in thought. "He really ought to get his own bike if he wants to survive that triathlon. My mountain bike's too heavy."

Tyler's eyes bugged out, eyebrows bristled, and with his imposing height and sun-lined, sharp-featured face, Jesse was reminded of a startled gargoyle. The very same sharp features had Jesse thinking, not for the first time, whether Tyler had some Native blood in him. And if he did, what tribe? Silence reigned while Jesse studied his employer, and it took a good minute before his boss recovered from his surprise.

"What, is Gillen entering, too?" he asked.

SEBASTIAN Gillen, the second-in-command of Gillen Frozen Desserts Company and his father's heir-apparent, looked over the new product lineup with a frown. Everything was full-butterfat, as gooey as one could make it, dense and rich and expensive. He looked at the nutritional content first.

Swim…bike…run…

His thoughts drifted to Jesse, who used to love Gillen Ice Cream. He'd been partial to chocolate, which had always had the richest formulation. He knew the other man hadn't bought any since January. If it had been perhaps just a bit healthier…

It irked him that he was unable to enjoy the very products he was forced to sell. There must be a better way to make frozen confections. Still all-natural, but with less sugar, less fat… no lactose. That way even he might even be tempted to at least taste the stuff and see what all the hoopla was about.

"This is unacceptable," he said, lifting his eyes from the proposal.

The representative of the New Products division squirmed in his seat at the sudden and unexpected assessment. So did the marketing director.

"But Mr. Gillen, our market surveys indicate that the richest ice cream commands the highest price."

"True," the CEO nodded. "However, this should not only be about price anymore." He pointed to the products and their respective lists of ingredients. "A major competitor has a new product line out – they use only five ingredients. Five. No more. Have you tried it?"

The team members shook their heads.

"Neither have I, since I can't eat the stuff. However, I'm told it's rather good." He leaned back in his chair and eyed the ceiling as he thought which approach would create the least amount of controversy. He wanted to take Marketing out to the woodshed for not knowing their competition well enough, but if he wanted to promote a different line of thought, he had to make them believe it was their idea all along.

"We'll take a break while I send Paulette out to buy two pints of each flavor available at the nearest store. Then we'll have a tasting. I see absolutely no reason, for instance, why we should use corn syrup when they don't."

"Mr. Gillen, the corn syrup is necessary to soften the ice cream a bit and prevent crystallization issues." The food chemistry director looked uncomfortable as he uttered his statement.

"If others make do without corn syrup, so will we. I am no longer pleased by our product line," Sebastian said. "In fact, I am no longer pleased by our values. I believe it's time to make some changes in the way we do things around here." His words resonated through the small conference room, bouncing from wall to wall.

There. He'd said it. Sebastian didn't know what possessed him to speak so openly. He'd been cultivating his position with care for several years now, and all of a sudden his words were full of heat and discord. His team was made up of men almost twice his age. Younger men – and women – occupied more junior positions. He'd have never made it as far as he had if he weren't the CEO's son. Treading lightly took precedence to passion.

Our product's hurting people.

He thought of Jesse again and the demons that plagued him, the skeletons that were buried under stratified layers of spare electronics in his closet.

Jesse mattered, because Jesse was his friend.

Sebastian looked around the cream-colored room with its dark wood and brass plant holder by the window. He made eye-contact with each of the three people in the room. The poorly concealed emotions he read in their faces ranged from mild disappointment to outright rebellion.

He had no friends here. None at all. Just men who thought they should be the ones sitting in his chair. Something had to change, and Sebastian wasn't looking forward to the storm he saw brewing on the horizon.

JESSE kept a wary eye on Sebastian. He noted the tightened jaw, the tension around his eyes, the absent, distracted expression. Half a mile passed as they jogged; then, all of a sudden, Sebastian slowed down to a walk.

"Everything okay?" Jesse let a bit of concern seep into his voice. They walked side by side for a short while before he got a reply.

"I had a nasty meeting at work. In order to convince my team of the error of their ways, I had to send my assistant out to buy our competitor's ice cream."

"Oh yeah?" Jesse had meant his tone to show interest, but the word 'ice cream' made him uncomfortable—the way a bottle of whiskey affected a recovering alcoholic.

"Yes. I had to, in fact, taste test several brands fairly early in the day. Then I spent almost an hour in the bathroom. It's a miracle I made it for our run."

Jesse grinned. It was hard to picture the normally calm, collected Sebastian Gillen bent over a toilet, working his way through severe GI distress.

"It's not easy to make changes," Sebastian continued.

"Uh-huh?" Jesse prompted him on.

"I'm surrounded by hide-bound traditionalists who would rather have their teeth pulled than consider changing our business concept."

Jesse absorbed the information, taking special note of the bitter tone and the accompanying tension in Sebastian's shoulders.

"You're trying to change things?" he asked.

"Yes." Sebastian responded, somewhat tersely.

"Why?"

Sebastian took a lot longer to answer this time. They ran another half-mile segment and slowed to a fast walk in the time it took for the other man to respond.

"It's not working," Sebastian said finally, keeping his sentences short so he didn't lose his breathing rhythm. "When's the last time you bought Gillen, Jesse?"

Jesse tucked an errant strand of jet-black hair off his forehead and frowned, wondering at the apparent change in topic. "Not since December. You know why, too."

"Exactly. Do you miss it?"

Jesse thought a bit. He hated admitting to a weakness. He was pretty sure that missing his favorite ice cream didn't reflect well upon his character, but Sebastian was working through a problem at work. Jesse chose to go with the truth.

"Yeah. I miss it."

"Do you buy anything else as a substitute?" Sebastian asked.

Jesse hated being disloyal to Sebastian's brand. A question had been asked, however, and there was no good reason he shouldn't give his friend an honest answer.

"Well…only a few times," he admitted.

"What did you try?" Sebastian asked. "And was it any good?

You know I can't eat these things, so I'm genuinely curious as to your opinion."

Encouraged by feeling that he could be of use, Jesse expounded on his knowledge of reduced-fat ice creams, sherbets, and sorbets. As he finished giving Sebastian his assessment, however, he found himself making an unexpected announcement:

"If I wanted anything at all, it would be a better sports drink. Or, a sports drink freezer pop. When I want ice cream, I'll have ice cream. No big deal – it's just once a month nowadays, so I can have what I really want. But what really pisses me off is having to drink those artificially flavored sports drinks. They're gross, and over-priced, and taste so awful but I really need them after two hours of sweating. It beats eating those electrolyte gels–or popping salt pills."

They ran another half-mile segment, hurrying up so they could resume their conversation.

"So what would you like to be able to buy, Jesse?"

"If there was a healthy, electrolyte-rich ice pop, I'd dig that. Definitely."

A new, exciting tendril of intrigue interest and possibility slowed Sebastian's recovery pace to a slow walk.

"Really," he said.

"Yeah." Jesse broke stride and waited for him so they could stroll side by side. "If you look at the b-boards, lots of triathletes feel that way. Marathoners, too. You have to eat all this artificial shit to make it through a race, and you have to get your digestive system used to it ahead of time."

YOUR WISH is my command, Jesse.

Sebastian let a small smile blossom on his face. This had poten-tial. But his smile was quickly replaced by a slight frown as he real-ized that things weren't quite that simple. If his own development and marketing team resisted movement toward creating healthier ice creams, he didn't see how he could possibly entice them to launch a line of frozen athletic supplements. Such a product would run counter to their current corporate mission statement.

There had to be a way, though. At the very least it was worth investigating.

A WEEK passed. Sebastian had declared his wounds "healed enough," and Jesse was eager to follow him so they could get in the pool again and resume their swim schedule. Sebastian had juggled his work schedule as best as he could, and they were able to meet after work twice more to ride through the park.

Jesse enjoyed watching Sebastian. The grace he had in the water, however, didn't translate to his biking efforts just yet. He still had difficulties in balancing, and shifting gears didn't come naturally.

Unfortunately, neither did braking.

"Hill ahead, hill ahead!" Jesse yelled, frantic to reach the determined beginner riding ahead of him. Sebastian still adhered to the theory that pedaling fast would make the bicycle more stable, thus making it less likely that he would fall.

Reaching the brake levers, however, demanded an extra layer of coordination. The act required loosening the death grip he had on the handlebars and stretching two fingers far, far out to reach the metal levers and pull them in. To Jesse's dismay, Sebastian found this affected his balance just enough to throw him off. Thus, Sebastian was afraid to use his brakes.

Jesse watched him coast down the hill and lean into the turn on the bottom.

Good, no crash-landing this time.

He coasted down the hill, following the intrepid Sebastian and figuring he'd be scraping him off the asphalt path sometime soon. Jesse cut the turn with ease and emerged out of the trees by a small lake.

Just ahead of him, Sebastian flashed across a flat swath of black pavement.

An ideal area to brake.

Three kids on bikes zoomed out the other side, followed by mothers with strollers and a very young child on a tricycle.

The path was blocked.

No way around.

"Fuck!" Jesse hit the brakes, pulling off onto the lawn, and stopped. His gaze followed one Sebastian Gillen, heir-apparent to Gillen Frozen Desserts, as he launched his mountain bike off the smooth path.

He careened onto the grass that divided the crowded thoroughfare from the lake.

Jesse knew Sebastian wouldn't even try the brakes. The unfamiliar and bumpy grass had Sebastian holding onto the handlebars with a white-knuckled grip.

The lawn sloped toward the water.

Sebastian struggled for control. Jesse held his breath. If he just slowed down some, he'd swing back onto the path...

SPLASH.

Time seemed to stop. The mothers' voices rose in startled exclamation, and their road-hogging little kids dropped their bikes and ran toward the water's edge.

Jesse tried to jump off and help, forgetting, of course, that his right foot was still clipped in—and his right shoe was currently held fast. Unable to detach himself, he struggled to get free while rolling forward.

Dammit. Let. Go.

He fussed, trying to kick out of his clips while keeping the thin, slick racing tires upright on the wet grass.

His feet came free. His bike, too, was free. Jesse was focused on clipping out while eyeing Sebastian's thrashing in the lake. The soft bank of the lake appeared under his front wheel as though out of nowhere. He swerved, attempted to dismount - and splashed in, falling backward.

Cold.

Wet.

Not deep – but slick and slimy and gross underneath.

"Eww." Jesse managed to stand without slipping and falling back in. His expensive biking shoes were now stuck in the fine mud and silt of the lake bed. He turned toward Sebastian.

"You okay?"

"I don't see why you have to follow my swimming technique to the letter, Hightower," Sebastian answered in a peevish tone.

"Where you lead, I follow," Jesse shrugged with a grin, pulling his bike out of the mud. He lifted one foot. The mud released him with a sucking sound, his biking shoe hanging on by his toe. One tentative step ahead didn't do much for his balance. Barely standing, he lifted his other foot up and moved toward the bank, step by squishy, disgusting step.

He tossed his bike on the wet, grassy bank as gently as he could, hoping he didn't screw up his derailleur.

Climbing up the bank was so slick and muddy, the only way out was on his hands and knees.

Sebastian was out already, muddy and wet and regal. He measured Jesse with an unruffled glance.

"Surely this could have been avoided."

"Yeah, sure! Why didn't you use your brakes?"

There was a brief silence.

"There is no point in entering a race you don't intend to win. Speed was of the essence."

Jesse rolled his eyes. He loved this guy. He loved the way he put on an air of total superiority while wet and dripping mud and while not addressing the fact that he was too much of a klutz to use the brake levers properly.

It wasn't like Sebastian was trying to be funny, but Jesse found his stoic approach hilarious. When Sebastian smiled, it was for real, warm and sunny and all-encompassing.

Jesse bent down to stand his bike up, averting his face as he tried to hide it.

He was a goner. He had fallen for this man – a friend who was way out of his league. A guy who was probably straight anyway. He'd been stupid to let himself fall hopelessly in love with a man as unattainable and perfect as Sebastian Gillen, and he didn't know what to do about it.

CHAPTER 7

"I NEED YOU to entice your new friend to visit us, Hightower," Tyler had growled, a wicked smile lighting up his features.

"Sure, boss. But don't you have his number?"

"I do, but if you tell him to please come over, he actually will."

Jesse mused over the request his boss had made two days ago. Tyler was right– it was almost certain that Sebastian would show up if Jesse asked. Especially after yesterday's biking disaster. Sebastian's effort to hose down the bikes in the alley next to the apartment building had been much appreciated, although his contrition had been unnecessary.

"They're just bikes. They're waterproof. As long as we get the silt out of the derailleurs and chains, they'll be okay." Jesse spoke in the most patient voice he was able to produce. It was just dirt. He'd seen dirt before– although it was quite apparent that the junior 'Leader of Industry' was quite unaccustomed to it.

"This is a good chance to scrub the chains. We're already wet and dirty." Jesse produced a bucket he'd gotten out of his basement storage unit, along with a bottle of cleanser. "Here, detergent. You drizzle it onto the chain as the rear wheel spins, see? Get some in the spokes. And use a toothbrush… I just use my old one… if you let it sit for ten minutes or so, the grime'll come off right quick." He put action to words and treated his bike, then passed the bottle to Sebastian. "Your turn."

Sebastian tried. That much was obvious. It was also quite clear he wasn't mechanically inclined. "Sorry," he mumbled for a ninth time.

"Well, ideally, we'd have them up on a bike stand. Or on a car's bike carrier. People do that to get the crud out of the drive train. It keeps the parts working longer and reduces resistance, but you need to use the right lube..."

Sebastian, who'd been listening with rapt attention, broke into a bout of coughing.

"Y'okay?" Jesse spared him a glance. Sebastian only nodded. A faint blush tinged his skin, making his few pale freckles disappear.

Just a friend, Jesse reminded himself. But damn if Sebastian didn't look hot when he blushed like that!

SEBASTIAN wheeled the clean, wet bike into the elevator right behind Jesse. The car was barely big enough for them to fit. He took in the old, fake wood paneling that had the 70's written all over them, the beat-up steel door, and the graffiti on the walls. They got out on the eighth floor. Sebastian hung a left, following Jesse down a dimly-lit hallway. The walls were covered with plastic wainscoting and painted a bilious green, and the gray carpet was one of those industrial ones companies used in their lobbies.

Jesse stopped and unlocked the three locks on his apartment's cream-colored door. "Let me get a towel real quick," he said with a note of apology. "The bikes..."

Of course. The bikes. Sebastian gave him an indulgent smile. For a man who sold his car to buy an expensive racing bike when he already had a perfectly serviceable one, his concern was certainly understandable. Unlike Sebastian, Jesse didn't have a trust fund that he could access freely in a couple of years.

Jesse came out with a faded beach towel and gave the bikes a thorough wipe-down. "Come on in," he said, leading the way.

Sebastian looked around the small space, conscious of the chaos they were adding to an already cluttered space.

"We need to clean up, too," Jesse said, stripping off his soaked hoodie and T-shirt, wiggling out of his sweat pants. "How about you strip and shower while I make hot tea. Or coffee? I'll get you some dry clothes."

"I'll have what you're having." Sebastian stripped naked by the door, leaving a pile of wet clothes on the vinyl tile entry pad.

"This way…"

"I remember, thank you." Jesse wasn't ogling him– was he? Yet Sebastian felt Jesse's curious eyes on his muddy, wet, and very naked back. It felt good, being looked up and down with no expectation of social favors or business introduction. When he got to the bathroom, a glance in the mirror above the sink showed a noticeable blush warming his face.

JESSE EYED the slim, pale athlete's nude form from behind. It was only a few steps into his small bathroom, but it was enough to feast his eyes on the perfect proportions, to caress the smooth skin with his gaze. Once Sebastian disappeared and the water came on, Jesse shook his head, confused. He'd seen him naked in the pool's showers more than once. The way he regarded him had changed, though, as though Sebastian was something precious and sublime.

He's gorgeous, like a statue in a museum.

That, however, didn't do Sebastian and his warm sense of humor justice. Not a cold marble statue - he was far from cold and unfeeling. Jesse worried his blossoming feelings like a sore tooth, cautiously probing, afraid of an almost inevitable jolt of pain.

He's really nice…I think he likes me.

Why else would he hang out with me?

The thought of 'liking' and 'being liked' led Jesse to wonder whether Sebastian liked him 'that way'.

Jesse took a quick internal inventory. Sebastian had, to date, been helpful, encouraging, and kind. He avoided embarrassing Jesse with that whole energy bar hoarding incident and he never once mentioned their difference in income or education or physical condition.

He'd been willing to try new things. Bicycles, for instance. Jesse replayed the ridiculous scene by the lake, the alarmed faces of the mothers and the glee of their children. Most of all, there was Sebastian and his dry humor.

And they talked about work, a bit about family, and lots about working out. They were getting to know one another, and the more Jesse learned, the more he hoped Sebastian might like him 'that way.'

Yet for once Jesse didn't seem to mind growing close to another man. He'd always minded before, ever since he'd been forced to live in a foster home where he'd been told that if he wanted to eat, he would have to sell his body to whomever his foster dad brought in.

Jesse had done his best to stay alone and single, away from cute guys and their sleek bodies. He'd seen a lot, and he managed to escape from it. Besides, being noticed for being a pretty boy had brought him only grief so far.

Although Sebastian might have noticed him.

That was a problem.

Wasn't it?

JESSE BANISHED these thoughts. They used to have their use, sure, but they were ancient history, and now he had a new problem to worry about. He had a naked guest in the shower – one whose clothes were muddy and soaking wet.

He opened his closet and reached for a pile on the upper left. It was his 'skinny clothes' pile from years ago, and since he had the space, he never saw a reason to throw those things away. He rifled through the pants and shirts, finally settling on a pair of gray stone-washed jeans, a black t-shirt, and a flannel button-down in a blue and green plaid. Jesse fished out a pair of clean socks from his drawer. No underwear, though. His would be too big – and sharing underwear might be construed as a bit... weird.

SEBASTIAN emerged from the shower clean and warm. His eyes drifted to the dry pile of clothing left on the closed lid of the toilet. Looking through the stack, he noted that Jesse had brought him everything he would need—save underwear.

Resigned, he made do without, dressing in the comfortable, broken-in clothes and finger-combing his towel-dried hair.

"All yours, Jesse!" he yelled out, emerging from the bathroom. "Thank you."

Jesse nodded with a smile and disappeared into the bathroom. Sebastian rounded up their muddy, sodden clothing into a plastic shopping bag, hoping there was a laundry in the basement of the building. Then he put up water to heat and searched the kitchen cabinets for two mugs and tea bags. Both of them could use a cup of something hot on the inside.

Jesse emerged in short time, dressed in black cargo pants and a cream-colored sweater. The stark black of his long, unruly hair looked dull while wet. Brush in hand, he fought to untangle the snarled locks while pacing around the small living room.

"Having some trouble, Jesse?" Sebastian asked over his cup of tea, his eyebrow raised fraction of an inch.

"It was the mud. My hair always tangles when I have to scrub it real hard."

"Don't you have detangler?"

"What's that?" Jesse had just about growled in frustration.

Sebastian set aside his cup of tea, patting the cushion beside him.

"Come. Sit here," he said.

Sebastian lifted himself up to the back of the sofa, perching with his feet planted wide on the cushions. Jesse hesitated for a moment, but Sebastian waited patiently, so Jesse finally resigned himself to his fate and did as he was asked, seating himself between Sebastian's knees. He relinquished the brush as Sebastian pushed at his back, urging him to lean forward, and set to detangling the sodden mess of his long hair.

"A DETANGLER is a hair product, usually a spray. It makes the hair shafts slippery so they don't tangle. My sister uses it." Jesse heard Sebastian's soothing voice as he worked his wet strands from the ends up. "And if your hair's wet, use a comb."

He felt his fingers stroke over his scalp as he separated the strands and brushed them, section by section. His hands were smaller than Jesse's, but strong and warm. He could feel the warmth of Sebastian's legs against his shoulders and felt the heat within him respond, building up in his core like an ancient fire that had been banked for way too long. Jesse felt his eyes begin to droop but he didn't fight it. He only leaned forward more, feeling Sebastian's nimble fingers run through his drying tresses, brushing them strand by strand, from bottom to the top.

So comfortable…

"Lean back a little."

Jesse let himself be guided backwards, cradled between Sebastian's thighs. The bike ride, the cold bath in the pond, and the hot shower added up all at once in a great wave of fatigue. He leaned back further. Now the back of his head rested against Sebastian's crotch. The contrast of its heat against his drying hair was enticing. Sebastian didn't seem to mind, so Jesse didn't fight it, even when his breath hitched a bit. Eyes closed, he only felt.

A few comfortable minutes later, Sebastian pushed him forward and begun to arrange the brushed strands up and behind.

"What're you doin'?"

"I am braiding your hair."

"Oh."

AS HE BRUSHED the silky jet-black hair, Sebastian observed Jesse's reaction to their close contact. He didn't flinch away from his touch at all. In fact, he did just the opposite. When he leaned back at his urging, his thighs giving support to Jesse's broad shoulders, Sebastian smiled in satisfaction when Jesse's dark eyes shuttered nearly closed in peaceful repose.

The hair was braided and tied off, but neither man showed any indication of wanting to move.

Maybe just a little bit more…

Feeling brave, Sebastian moved his fingers back to the temples and massage the skin with his fingertips in a row of small circles along the hairline. He saw Jesse bite back the tiniest gasp, and smiled, rubbing the circles down the sides of his head, behind his ears…

Maybe I could try this…

He pressed his thumbs into the strong, hard muscles in the back of Jesse's neck. One on each side of the spine, erector spinae extended from the base of the skull all the way down to the small of the back. Sebastian always found neck-rubs to be incredibly relaxing, and he smiled with satisfaction as Jesse began to melt under his fingers. He let out an occasional whimper—sometimes in surprise, sometimes in pleasure, sometimes in pain. The small, barely audible exhalations told Sebastian whether he should press harder or ease up, stay on the spot or move on.

"That just feels too good," Jesse said many minutes later, his voice faintly tinged with embarrassment.

"It's supposed to," the other man replied calmly, ignoring his flustered feelings. He didn't want to make his friend uncomfortable.

A few more strokes up Jesse's neck and then he stopped, reluctantly pulling his hands away from the honey-gold skin. "You should feel more comfortable now. Drink some water; the body requires it after a massage. If you feel somewhat congested afterwards, don't worry—it's perfectly normal."

"How do you know all this?" Jesse asked, voice drowsy and content.

"Many years of training," he answered, striving to keep his tone light.

Could have been training for the Olympics.

Sebastian bit back the bitter thought.

"I should go. I need to get home and you need to go to sleep," he said finally, when Jesse showed no sign of moving. He really didn't want to go.

"Okay. I'll do the laundry and give it to you later." Jesse yawned, still not moving.

"You sure?" Sebastian hesitated, then set his hands on the strong shoulders that emanated so much warmth.

"Sebastian?"

"Yes, Jesse."

"Can I ask you for a favor?"

"Yes."

Anything. Well, almost anything.

"Would you come visit me at work tomorrow?"

The pale hands tightened on Jesse's shoulders.

"Why?"

"Tyler asked me to ask you. It doesn't seem to be business related."

Sebastian Gillen thought a bit. "Well, we are using his security system. I don't see why I couldn't go and find out more about his newest upgrades."

"Thank you."

"You don't know what he wants?"

"No, but he said if I asked you, you'd be more likely to come."

The admission came naturally. Sebastian smiled and let his hands run up and down Jesse's shoulders, finally detaching himself and swinging his legs off the back of the sofa so he could stand on the floor and away from Jesse. If he didn't, he would never leave.

"I'll see you tomorrow, then."

Jesse got up and rotated his neck around until it cracked. "Thanks," he said. "That felt great. Maybe I could do this for you someday?"

Sebastian swallowed. Hard. "Maybe. I think I'd like that."

They stood by the door for some time, silent, suddenly uncertain how to say goodbye. Finally, Sebastian nodded and offered a quick, warm smile, which Jesse returned, and he let himself out, reluctant to leave the other man and his crowded apartment behind for the empty loneliness of his own, far-too-large home across town.

SEBASTIAN'S laundry was in the dryer for the night, the door was locked, and Jesse was finally in bed. As he snuggled under his comforter, his mind replayed the sensation of Sebastian Gillen's skilled, gentle hands in his hair, on his head, up and down his neck. The pleasure was still there – he could tap into his memories to reach it and feel its echo over and over again.

I wish he could have stayed…

His conscious mind didn't even register the thought as he drifted asleep.

CHAPTER 8

THE PHONE went off the moment Jesse grabbed another handful of tissues.

"Hello?" he croaked.

"Jesse. It's Sebastian."

"Hi, Sebastian," he replied in a nasal monotone.

"Do you want me to come over after our run?" The calm, smooth voice inquired from several buildings away.

Jesse paused. The idea of running sat ill with him all of a sudden and he stammered, not knowing what to say.

"Jesse, are you alright?"

"Sure," Jesse blurted out his automatic answer. He was always all right... wasn't he? He'd gotten to work, after all. He didn't fall off his bike twice, even though it was a close call with his ears clogged the way they had been that morning. "Of course I'm fine. Yeah, come over after the run. I'll tell the boss."

Jesse hung up his phone and leaned back in his computer chair. His head felt heavy and dense, ears popping and voice threatening to break as though he was a mutating teenage boy all over again. He blew his nose again.

He really, really didn't want to run. He wanted to snuggle down in the lounge with a cup of hot soup from the vending machine and read a magazine. If it were a training magazine, he could at least read about other people running. That would make him feel less guilty. Training research was, after all, just as important as training itself.

Wasn't it?

JESSE GLARED at the screen. The windows and symbols looked all wavy and blurry. Damn piece of Korean junk. How could a high-definition screen act like an old tube? Preposterous. He blinked hard, forcing himself to focus, and set up routine systems checks. Those would take their time running, chewing data, and weeding out spare fragments of obsolete applications.

Jesse heaved his stiff body out of the chair and walked over to Tyler Easton's office. The door was open. He knocked on the doorframe and waited for his boss to lift his head.

"Yeah?" he said. "Come in, Jesse."

Jesse sauntered in and sank into the client chair, slumping against the padded backrest.

"Sebastian will visit after lunch."

"You eat together, too?" Tyler asked, raising his sharp eyebrow. His eyes were cold and brown and piercing. Those, together with his broken beak of a nose, reminded Jesse of a hawk. He wondered what his totem animal would be, had Tyler even gone on a vision quest.

"Nah… we're running again." He tried not to sniffle as his congested voice barely made its way out of his throat.

His boss leaned back in his executive desk chair and looked him up and down with his keen gaze.

"Straighten up. Slumping won't make you feel any less sick." The gravelly voice irritated Jesse, making him sit up and stare at Tyler with a baleful glare.

"I ain't sick. Just tired."

"Asshole. Of course you're sick and you're here just spreading germs. Why didn't you call in sick and stay home?"

"I have work to do." And there was no way in hell Jesse would risk his job by calling in sick. Calling in sick meant getting fired eventually, getting fired meant having to live on the streets again, living on the streets meant…

"Hightower!" Tyler barked. "What the fuck's wrong with you, man? You're spacing out on me. I'm asking, what's your rest day?"

Jesse blinked. His eyelids felt uncommonly heavy as he struggled to focus his bleary gaze on his boss. Tyler stood behind his desk and stretched his tall, formidable frame. He was wearing a black polo shirt with the 11th Hour Security logo just like everyone else did, claiming it was more practical than white work shirts – those needed to be ironed. His broad shoulders filled the polo to its breaking point, the muscular outline of those shoulders, his chest, and his lats visible even under the heavy, opaque fabric. He was older than Jesse – even older than Sebastian – yet he remained in amazing physical condition. He could run circles around most of his much younger employees.

"What do you mean, 'rest day'?"

Tyler sighed. "Look, there's the triathlon I made y'all do, and you're obviously training. That's good. You're diligent and determined, and that's good, too." Jesse's heart warmed at the words of praise, but the warm fuzzies didn't last long. "You look a bit less like the soft computer-jockey I hired and more like the security specialist you are," Tyler went on. "So all right, you're focused. I dig that. But you might be overtraining. Once a week, pick any day, you need to take a break. It's called a 'rest day'. That means no training. Just stretch out, go for a little walk, get more sleep."

Jesse stirred. The idea of not training one day a week filled him with a sense of apprehension.

"But then I won't make progress as fast."

"If you over-train and get hurt, you'll have to sit out for a few weeks, which is even worse." Tyler gave him a serious look. "No running today. Just walk, if you must. Take a rest day, kid."

Tyler turned his back on him and looked out the window. He was so huge, his silhouette had almost filled the window itself. His hair was slicked back into a long ponytail and held with a yellow rubber band with two pink plastic daisies on it. Courtesy of Tyler's daughter, no doubt. Little Yasmine was a tiny pink-clad terror of only eleven years of age and Jesse secretly enjoyed the days she came to the office after school. She had a way of livening up the office and making things… interesting.

SEBASTIAN'S brow furrowed in concern. First Jesse's congested voice, now a call saying he'd rather just walk today. He didn't mind skipping a run – he could lift weights once he got home.

He didn't bother changing. Leaving the office with his phone and his wallet would be enough today.

Jesse was already waiting outside. Something light and unexpected fluttered in his stomach when he saw that honest smile split Jesse's face. He pushed his way away from the steel jamb of rotating door of his office building. The black work uniform of cargo pants and a polo shirt suited him well. His only concession to the early spring chill was a battered green windbreaker. His hair spilled loose over his shoulders, unbound and lush. Sebastian felt the ground lose substance, and his world become weightless as he recalled brushing it out for him only the night before.

Soft and strong. Like silk.

"Hey… sorry to wimp out," Jesse said, glancing at Sebastian's black suit, white shirt and pale green tie.

"Don't worry about it. You sound like you might be coming down with something." Sebastian's reply was choked as he turned his head to loosen his tie and undo his top button. "It's probably from us falling into that lake yesterday and walking home in wet clothes. You should rest if you're sick." He looked Jesse up and down. His naturally bronzed skin looked a bit ashen today, and there were circles under his eyes.

"I'm not sick. Why does everyone think I'm sick?" Jesse bit off, sounding a lot sharper than he probably intended.

Sebastian raised his eyebrows. Not many took that tone with him, yet he found Jesse's boldness refreshing. He pressed his lips together, determined not to let his amusement show. "Whatever you say. Let's go out to lunch? My treat."

THEY SETTLED at one of only four tables at a small eatery called Bistro DiRoy halfway between the office complex and the baseball stadium that fronted the confluence of the Allegheny and the Monongahela, where the mighty Ohio River was born. The place had a good lunch selection, and they baked their own bread. Sebastian opted for a grilled beef salad full of exotic greens.

Jesse moped over the menu for some time. Finally, he settled for a bowl of chicken noodle soup. Sebastian snorted.

"What?" Jesse looked up, only to see Sebastian pick the candied walnuts out of his salad and set them to the side of his plate.

"Jesse… it's a beautiful, sunny spring day, yet you chose a hot soup, and you're still wearing that jacket."

"So?"

He reached across the table and touched Jesse's sweaty forehead.

"Hmmm. If you had a fever, it has already broken."

Jesse froze. Nobody had ever touched his forehead to see if he had a fever. Not even his foster grandmother had done that. She relied on the numbers yielded by her thermometer instead. He didn't remember being sick as a small child. What did his mother do back then? And after his father took him off the reservation, there had been the military base and an infirmary with its no-nonsense white walls and shiny chrome implements and vaccination needles.

For the first time in his life, Jesse felt a hand extend to his face in a gesture of concern.

Not even Caleb…

They had been each other's best friends, only friends. They had crossed the continent together, yet despite having each other's back, Caleb had never been the touchy-feely nurturing type. Jesse didn't know why it bothered him now when he had never questioned it back then.

"Jesse." Warm, gray eyes watched him from underneath long, graceful eyelashes. "What's the matter?"

Jesse looked up, and a long moment went by before something shifted in his eyes – resolve flickering over his face as he squared his shoulders and blew out a deep breath.

"You're so kind… you know… to give a damn about how I feel."

The honest words took Sebastian by surprise.

"Of course I care. It is customary to care for those you l – care for."

For those you love.

Sebastian bit his tongue to keep the "L" word inside. The timing would have been spot-on, but the word scared him. He liked Jesse. No – he loved Jesse, but telling him could cost him the other man's friendship and, having become accustomed to his comforting presence, he didn't think he could live with himself if he chased Jesse away.

HALF an hour later they took the elevator up to Jesse's office instead of running up the stairs the way they would have usually done. Jesse opened the door for him.

"Nel, would you tell Tyler that Sebastian Gillen is here?"

The woman named Nel smiled at him over the reading glasses that sat on her freckled nose.

"Sure, Jesse," she chirped in her sunny voice and picked up the phone to dial Tyler's extension. A mischievous smile developed as she listened to her boss' voice booming over the receiver. Jesse could hear the sound, but not the content.

"Okay, boss," she said. She hung up and turned her wide, stormy eyes to meet Sebastian's with feigned innocence.

"Would you please wait here in the lobby?" she asked, then gestured toward the chairs lined against one wall. "Have a seat!"

"This is highly irregular," Sebastian intoned, but Jesse shushed him.

"I'll wait with you, since I'm the one who invited you up." Then he reached behind Nel's partition and snagged a handful of tissues to blow his nose once again.

DESPITE the playful side he chose to reveal to Jesse, most of the time, Sebastian Gillen was a man of gravitas. He seldom permitted himself excessive displays of anger—or joy. The same lack of social skills that had been the death-knell of his social life on the playground turned out to be an asset in both business and family negotiations. Therefore, when he saw the 11th Hour Security employees trickle into the lobby and line up by the walls, his expression retained a practiced, bored facade of calm.

Jesse, on the other hand, glanced from face to face, not liking this at all. Tyler was going to pull some stupid stunt, Sebastian would be humiliated in public by a seemingly innocent prank, and their friendship would cool off. Few things felt more threatening to Jesse than losing Sebastian's comforting presence by his side.

TYLER FINALLY arrived, filling more than his allotted space with his presence alone.

"Mr. Gillen!" He grinned a toothy grin at Sebastian, who stood in greeting. The two men shook hands and, to his shock, Jesse watched them squeeze each other's hand harder and harder, like a pair of idiotic teenagers jockeying for position. Neither man's expression changed.

The rest of the team watched the exchange with gleeful grins from the sidelines. Jesse noticed small bills changing hands as the two stopped squeezing their metacarpals into submission, and finally let go. Sebastian's smaller, fine-boned hand stood up to the grip of Tyler's paw rather admirably. The whole company must have been running one of those bets, Jesse realized, and smiled. If that had been all, then perhaps Sebastian could discuss business and leave and everything would be all right.

Except Tyler wasn't done. He nodded to Jazz, a fine-boned and a rather beautiful brunet just a bit shorter than Sebastian, who ducked into a nearby conference room only to wheel out a brand-new, top of the line road bike.

"It's my understanding, Sebastian, that you and Jesse are

training partners for the triathlon in August." Tyler gave
Sebastian his full-out, feral grin. His eyes blazed, his nostrils flared,
his pointy teeth dripped with saliva and Jesse had a sudden and
inexplicable feeling that somehow, a wind had begun to gather
within the lobby. He wiped a trickle of cold sweat off his brow with
the sleeve of his windbreaker.

"I've also heard that you've been most helpful to my key IT
guy in his swimming efforts, and in turn he got you into cycling.
Now, I know how particular you are about your equipment," he
gave Sebastian a significant look, which harkened to their long and
mysterious history. "Only the best for you, Sebastian."

Tyler waved at Jazz, who handed the curved handlebars of the
bicycle to Sebastian.

He accepted it with hesitation. This was no ordinary bike, but a
serious racing machine equipped with small, high-end
components. Its promise of athletic prowess made an interesting
contrast with Sebastian in his executive uniform of suit and tie.

He stroked its sleek racing frame. It was a pearlescent white,
strewn with little pink blossoms and the occasional pale-green leaf.
White and gray mingled with black and silver, and with that exotic
floral flush it looked unapologetically girly.

Sebastian knew quality when he saw it. The colors should have
offended him, but...

"Thank you, Ty." Sebastian met Tyler's gaze with calm appreciation. "I see you remember my favorite hobby of gardening. It's truly
lovely. Unfortunately I do not have the background to appreciate
this fine bicycle. If you would...?"

Jesse stared, sensing the obvious and immediate energy crack-
ling between his boss and his new friend.

"Yes. With pleasure." Tyler's hand skimmed Sebastian's elbow
in a gesture that was almost courtly as he took the bike from him
and lifted it on one finger.

"This bike weighs only seventeen pounds and three ounces.
That makes it race-legal. Bikes have to weigh at least fifteen pounds
in most races nowadays. Now... let's see. The carbon fiber frame
is an obvious advantage – see? The components are all top-notch,

racing-quality. You have only six gears. Professional riders use five or less anyway and there's no use weighing the bike down with extra hardware. The brakes have bigger pads than usual, just to make sure. The derailleur is exposed, so don't toss it in the back of your car and screw it up. And, I had them put your clip pedals on. Where the hell are those shoes?"

Tyler looked around – somebody handed him a shoebox.

"I still remember your size." He grinned at Sebastian. "In fact, I believe the bike is customized to fit your body perfectly." Tyler's voice was a satisfied purr now.

AN UNREASONABLE wave of irritation swept over Jesse as he watched his boss adjust the painfully narrow racing seat for Sebastian. His jaw clenched and teeth ground together at the sight of Tyler's hands on Sebastian's hips, steadying him on the precarious bicycle with only the tips of his shoes touching the ground.

A wave of anger directed toward his boss washed over him. It was hot and red and seething, and it needed to get out, somehow, somewhere–but not here. Not at work.

I'm gonna tear you in half if you touch 'im again.

The thought arrested him. Jesse froze. He was gripped by jealousy, an insane and overwhelming wave of possessiveness toward Sebastian who looked so fine, so sexy, and was so kind. Who took him out to lunch and swam and ran and biked with him. Who didn't mind sleeping over in his slummy little apartment. He felt possessive of Sebastian, who just possibly might swing his way, but who was also entirely out of his league.

Tyler's hand slipped below Sebastian's waist.

Jesse saw Sebastian stiffen as Tyler invaded his physical space further. There was nowhere to go – Sebastian was stuck straddling the narrow machine.

"That's enough, Ty." The cold voice of Sebastian Gillen cut through the air. Jesse expected his boss to back off, but Tyler pinched the rounded bottom instead. Nobody else could have seen it because of the way they were angled.

Sebastian didn't react.

Jesse launched himself out of his seat, two quick steps taking him to his boss' side. He grabbed his shoulder and yanked, making Tyler's broad frame turn around.

"He says that's enough, boss."

An eyebrow rose. "Did he now?" Tyler's other hand slid down Sebastian's stranded thigh, his gaze locked with Jesse's heated glare.

Jesse punched him.

Someone gasped.

He landed a right hook, hitting Tyler right on the chin. The impact of fist against rock-hard jaw hurt like hell. Jesse sucked in some air and hung his arm by his side, surreptitiously straightening and closing his fingers.

He wasn't going to cradle his hand in public. He wasn't.

It had been a good punch. Jesse had twisted his right foot into it, from the ground-up, the way his Dad had taught him. Now he felt he should say something, anything, to break the deadly silence that had descended on the whole group. Shocked faces swam at the periphery of his vision, but his only focus was his taller, stronger, and much tougher boss.

"Well, well, well. Look who's sticking up for the Princess."

"Ty. That's enough." Sebastian's cool, smooth voice sliced through the suddenly thick air. He tilted the bike to the side and managed to get off, awkward and uncertain. He beckoned Jazz to hold it as he stepped up to his benefactor.

"It was very kind of you to think of me. Very generous of you as well. This gift is so extravagant... it's like giving a spirited stallion to a brand new rider. But I won't let you down. I will use it in the triathlon and do well on it. It is, beyond any doubt, well up to my exacting standards."

Jesse felt that chill in the air again and shivered in his zipped-up jacket. The way those two locked their gazes was unnerving. They knew one another well – very well indeed – and the knowledge rankled.

Sebastian turned to Jesse. His expression of calm determination changed to one of concern.

"You don't look well, Jesse." His hand reached to his cheek and smooth, pale fingers stroked hot skin. "I believe your fever has returned."

"I told you not to come to work if yer sick," Tyler added with a growl. "Go home and get well. Sergio, go get Jesse's stuff."

Jesse fought a sudden impulse to hang his head. He straightened up and lifted his chin, looking the taller Tyler right in the eyes. "I'm fired. Okay. I guess I deserve that." He didn't say he was sorry, though, and he wasn't going to beg. Begging never came easy to him.

Tyler returned his stare. There was no malice in it. Curiosity, maybe. Poorly hidden amusement, too. "Nah... I think I'll keep you around for a while. You earn your keep in entertainment value alone."

Jesse looked around with alarm clearly written over his face. "Just... just entertainment?"

"You do good work, but don't let it get to your head, kid." There was an irritated growl in Ty's voice now. "Go. Let Sebastian take you home."

"But... but my bike..."

"I'd rather you didn't bike, Jesse. I'll give you a ride." Sebastian turned to Tyler. "I'll leave my new bike here with Jesse's and pick them up later. If that's acceptable to you."

"Sure thing, Princess." Tyler's voice was, once again, leavened with amusement. "And tell your boyfriend not to get so damn protective of you next time around."

THE HEATED bucket seat of the Audi felt awfully snug and comfortable as Jesse settled in. It made his eyes feel heavy, his breathing evened out, and it wasn't till they got halfway to Jesse's apartment that he opened his mouth, his voice coming out as an uncertain croak.

"He... he called you my boyfriend."

"Hmm." Sebastian glanced away from the road, meeting Jesse's feverish, stunned gaze. "Would that bother you?"

Jesse whipped his head toward the driver, eyes glazed over. "N... no."

Jesse caught a glance of Sebastian's soft, gray eyes. His expression spelled relief, closely followed by cautious optimism. Sebastian cleared his throat and changed the topic.

"That's a beautiful bicycle. You'll have to teach me how to ride it."

The statement brought enough heat into Jesse's voice to match the fever apparent in his face.

"Are you kidding? That fucking asshole! He was mocking you, Sebastian. He was getting inside your space and he was setting you up for a huge embarrassment. He – he's always been such a fucking bag of stinkin' monkey shit! He does that all the time, all nice and generous on the surface, but underneath he's laughing at you. At everybody."

The outburst was met with only two quiet words. "I know."

"You know? And you put up with it?"

"He and I go way back, Jesse. Tyler and I lived together when we were at Wharton."

"He went to Wharton?" Jesse hissed. His surprised exclamation was followed by an immediate, "Wait… what do you mean, you 'lived' together?"

Sebastian sighed. "Just that. We were together… then he dropped out of school and we broke up."

The rest of the drive back to Jesse's apartment passed in silence.

SEBASTIAN allowed himself a small smile of relief as he checked the thermometer again.

101.5 Fahrenheit – much better than half an hour ago.

Jesse was asleep on top of his bed, still fully dressed save for his shoes. His black work uniform was soaked with the sweat of his fever breaking. His congestion wasn't obstructing his breathing, so Sebastian placed the thermometer on the crowded nightstand. It was time to do a bit of exploration.

Half an hour later, he had finished diving into Jesse's

jam-packed closet and had assembled two sets of pajamas, along with two more sets of clean sheets. He discovered a Gatorade mix in the pantry, along with an assortment of canned soups. The refrigerator contained milk, eggs, two kinds of cheese, and a bag of apples. The emptiness of Jesse's pantry took Sebastian by surprise. Gone were the candy bars, athletic bars posing as health food, the excess boxes of pasta and jars of sauce. The small freezer was devoid of leftovers wrapped in tidy squares of aluminum foil. Only a plastic bin of ice cubes remained.

Something had changed.

Or, rather, Jesse had changed.

"If you can afford to buy it, you can afford to throw it out."

Sebastian recalled how his very words had shocked the grin off Jesse's face weeks ago, yet Jesse must have reconsidered the principle of the matter. The barren cupboards didn't help Sebastian with his plan, however. With a resigned sigh, he fished the phone out of the pocket of his suit trousers and dialed a number.

"Yolanda. I need a hand. I'm at Jesse's and I'll need some cooking ingredients... sure, I'll text the list over to you. Here's the address."

His next call was to work, alerting his secretary that something had come up and he would be working from a remote location.

The last number he dialed was listed under "Doctor-family." He clicked on the contact and navigated the complex voice-mail menu before he could punch in the number of his physician's private extension.

"Dr. Grant, Sebastian Gillen speaking. I have a new patient for you... Yes, a house call would be appreciated. Let me give you the address."

As soon as he hung up, his phone rang. He lowered the volume, sighing at familiar ring tone and eyeing the caller ID with resignation.

Renata.

"Yes, Renata." His monotone betrayed none of his impatience.

"Seb? What's going on?"

"What do you mean? Be specific."

"Well…" He could tell she was working hard to quell her impatience. Her voice was now schooled into sweet concern. "I called Paul, and he said you told your secretary you'd be gone for the rest of the day. Is everything all right?"

"Yes. You have nothing to worry about."

"Where are you?"

Sebastian sighed. Ever since the row with the Board of Directors over the new product line, his sister had been after him, trying to monitor his every move, trying to question his every decision. She wanted to make sure he didn't antagonize the family, she'd said. Her nosiness was never a welcome thing. She'd been a lot more pleasant when her sole concern had been her yoga class and her evening social engagements.

"I'm taking care of some personal business."

The silence on the line grew louder and louder.

"Will you be home for dinner?" she said, finally breaking the growing tension.

Sebastian had made a split-second decision. He could return home and then come back to check on Jesse – but then again, he could just stay and see to his needs until his fever dropped, as he'd originally planned.

"Now that you mention it, it's more practical for me to eat out. Let the cook know."

Renata's voice took on an agitated, irritated edge and Sebastian could just picture her flashing eyes, her diminutive stature growing with every word she uttered.

"You can't just do that."

"I am sure you think that." And he hung up. He looked at the cellular phone in his hand and realized he was gripping it so hard his knuckles were turning white.

A POUNDING headache woke Jesse up. He expected his loose hair to be a tangled mess and reached up to feel the disaster with his fingertips. There was no mare's nest, no knots and tangles and snares. Just finely brushed hair, plaited into a loose braid. Jesse recognized this fact as an aberration, which forced him to pry his eyes open.

The room was dark. Only the bathroom night-light cast an eerie glow across his bed through a crack in the door. Jesse sat up, searching his memory but not remembering whether or not he had left the light on.

He looked down. His work clothes were gone, even though he had no memory of taking them off. Now he was dressed in a pair of ancient pajamas worn soft by frequent launderings and the sheets on the bed were white, not striped brown like the ones he had put on last week. And he was feeling clean. The sickly sweat was gone and he felt a hundred times better than he had earlier – yet he had no recollection of having showered.

The apartment itself had an odd air to it, a scent he couldn't place, a slight noise that didn't belong. Somebody must have brought him home. Somebody...

Cozy, heated seats.

Warm eyes the color of summer storm clouds.

Sebastian.

Jesse rolled off his bed and stood up, cautious of his balance. He made use of the bathroom. A great thirst seized him, and he recalled the jar of Gatorade powder in the kitchen. Slowly, he padded along the floor, every step awakening the lingering headache he'd hoped had disappeared. The lights were on, as though somebody was still there.

The sense of wrongness increased. A fragrance of lemons and raspberries hung in the air, accompanied by the exotic scent of something sweet and biting, and ginger, and another scent he couldn't quite pinpoint. He was startled by the unexpected sound of breathing. He spun around, regretting the sudden movement as pain lanced through his head.

Across the room, curled up on the sofa, slept Sebastian. He was wrapped in a spare sheet and covered in one of the sleeping bags Jesse kept rolled up in the corner. His shorter body almost fit, but the way he was curled up made Jesse wince in sympathy at the stiffness he was sure to feel the next day. His face wasn't as pale as when they'd met in February, with more freckles on his nose and cheeks. The kiss of sunshine played well against the short waves of Sebastian's dark blond hair. His lips, normally so thin and tight, were plump and relaxed.

Jesse knelt, observing the man.

Boyfriend.

He had never considered himself in that light, mostly because he didn't feel worthy of someone like Sebastian. He'd been eyeing him, sure – that was hard to avoid – ever since they'd met. Every workout, every hour they had spent together, had only made Jesse's appreciation of Sebastian grow. Now, as he observed him in his sleep, he thought of the boyfriend comment, and of Sebastian's reaction to it.

He hadn't disputed it. On the contrary, he had said something in the car that might've been an indication of acceptance.

He was kind.

Interesting.

He was very, very beautiful.

Unbidden, Jesse's hand moved towards Sebastian's face and his fingers reached out to smooth an imaginary hair off his face. As his fingertips skimmed the skin of Sebastian's cheek, his sense of touch was overwhelmed by the other man's softness.

Soft, yet not soft. Tough as nails inside.

Tough enough to swim many miles a week, tough enough to match Tyler in a juvenile contest of strength.

His lips were parted, air trickling in and out, and Jesse was struck with a pressing need to kiss him. Those lips might be as soft as his cheeks, or they might be even softer. Not much could possibly compare to Sebastian's smooth skin.

Jesse's finger descended to the gentle arc of Sebastian's upper lip, touching lightly, gently brushing his finger over the Cupid's bow.

Even softer. Wow.

He smiled, but withdrew his hand when Sebastian's eyelashes quivered, as though he were about to wake.

CHAPTER 9

FONDLING an unwitting guest in his sleep was poor form. Jesse sighed, pushed an escaped wisp of long hair out of his face, and carefully straightened.

The smart thing to do would be to simply get something to drink and let Sebastian sleep. The microwave display showed it was 2:30 in the morning, and the inky darkness outside was broken only by streetlights eight floors below. Sebastian might not have planned on sleeping over, but it was far too late to wake him.

Jesse tiptoed into the kitchen as quietly as he could and clicked on the small light over the stove. He opened the cupboard and grasped one of his four drinking glasses, trying to be absolutely silent. The soft 'thud' of a cabinet door closing sounded like the blow of a hammer to his ears.

He froze, listening.

Sebastian didn't stir, and Jesse let out the breath he'd been holding. Slowly, he opened another cabinet door and peered inside, fuzzy-headed, slow to locate the familiar canister of Gatorade drink mix. As his fingers wrapped around its short, cylindrical shape, a slender hand grasped his wrist.

"You can do better than that," Sebastian said next to him, his voice a soft whisper.

Jesse startled, then slowly turned. He didn't expect to see Sebastian up.

"You should be sleeping," he said in an accusing, still-hushed tone.

Thin eyebrows rose. "So should you," Sebastian whispered in retort. "How're you feeling?"

Jesse thought for a while, taking an internal inventory of symptoms. "My knees hurt. And my back... my shoulders and wrists, too. I feel better, the fever's gone but I feel, hmm...off, y'know? Like I should be okay but there's something wrong."

Sebastian's gaze was serious. "Anything else?"

"I'm not hungry. I'm thirsty, though. And my head hurts, and the headache makes my stomach feel a bit off."

Sebastian felt his forehead with his soft, cool hands. "You have no fever now, but you are sweaty again. I need you to drink, and try to eat at least a little bit, and take another shower before the fever returns."

Jesse froze, then turned slowly. "What do you mean, another?"

Gray eyes twinkled with a hint of amusement. "You had been running a serious fever for the last three days and nights. Every time your fever broke, you'd sweat, so you had a quick, tepid bath. You seem well enough to shower on your own tonight, so do it while you still feel good."

"Three days?" Jesse raised his voice in shock. He didn't remember a thing. "This... this is some kind of a joke, right?"

"No joke, Jesse. It's Friday. Tyler knows you're sick. A doctor has been here to check on you twice. I am here with you, not only to help, but also under quarantine. You have the flu. I don't need to pass that onto my coworkers and family."

"And..." Jesse searched for words, concern filling his eyes. "And you're not sick?" He stepped away from the shorter man. "I don't want to infect you."

"I seem to be fine," Sebastian said, his voice a disinterested monotone. "I rarely get ill. Plus, I had my flu shot last fall." He spun toward the freezer. "You are thirsty and in need of electrolytes. I have a little surprise for you." He opened the thick door, pulling out a popsicle freezer pop mold.

"Would you like raspberry or lemonade?"

Jesse's eyes lit up. "Really? You got me Popsicles?"

"No. I made you ice pops. Like you had requested," Sebastian corrected with a mischievous smile. "They contain enough electrolytes to keep your body happy, and all of their ingredients still remember where they came from. Let me know if you find their taste acceptable." There was that wry tone again. How could anyone not find homemade freezer pops 'acceptable?'

Jesse smiled. "Raspberry," he decided after some hesitation. Sebastian ran warm tap water over the plastic mold, coaxing it to release the frozen treat. It took a bit of wiggling before it popped free. But within a minute or two, Jesse was seated in the living room with Sebastian's bedding tucked around him. His houseguest had turned on a lamp, its light dim and soothing in the otherwise dark room, and Jesse sat with his feet propped up on the coffee table, frozen raspberry treat in his hand. Sebastian sat down as well, his eyes trained on Jesse, awaiting his reaction.

JESSE'S LUSH, red lips enveloped the frozen cylinder. He closed his eyes and moaned with pleasure. Sebastian knew it was good – he'd already tasted one, and watching Jesse confirmed his own opinion. He knew the bright top notes of fresh raspberries were exploding in Jesse's mouth just about now, and he also knew the sweet and sour balance was perfect.

"Mmm… so good!" Jesse closed his eyes and sucked on the freezer pop hard, finally letting it slide out of his mouth with an audible pop. The sound stopped him in his tracks. Jesse cleared his throat and shifted in his seat, obviously aware of Sebastian's scrutiny. He glanced at him, a wry grin on his face.

"This is fucking incredible," he said. "It tastes like a dessert! How'd you do it?"

Sebastian swallowed dry, and shrugged. He didn't trust his voice not to break at the sight of Jesse enjoying what he had made for him, and presently his awareness centered on a growing problem below his waist.

"Come on, Sebastian. Don't make it like it's nothing," Jesse said. "Here, you gotta have one too." Jesse got up, returning in only a short while with one of the lemon popsicles, and handing it to him.

"I know sweets aren't your thing, but these aren't really sweet. They're tart and fruity, and there's some kind of spice in there. Definitely delicious, though."

Sebastian leaned against the back of the sofa and eyed the icy treat. He knew how it tasted – after all, he formulated its composition. He'd have no problem eating it if only Jesse weren't watching him.

"Sebastian, if you won't eat it, I'm gonna think you drugged it or something," Jesse jested, oblivious to both Sebastian's discomfort and his own melting cylinder of icy goodness.

"Oh all right. Since you insist." Sebastian resigned, hoping Jesse would be too focused on his own treat to pay him any mind.

Jesse looked at the red drips staining his fingers. "Crap! Can't waste something this good!" Without hesitation, he licked the leggy liquid off his wrist and fingers, running his slick, pointed tongue all the way up to the tip of the now much smaller shape.

He glanced over at Sebastian through long eyelashes. "It's gonna melt if you don't eat it," he said.

Sebastian couldn't walk away from this particular situation – not unless he wanted to advertise the severity of his physical condition.

He sighed. "All right then," he said and licked the lemony surface. The tart freshness of lemon, accompanied by a bite of fresh ginger and just the smallest hint of fragrant cardamom exploded across his tongue. Just as he had planned it days ago.

Not bad.

Sebastian let the frozen tip slip between his lips, and sucked.

JESSE'S EYES widened at the sight. He now knew how soft those lips were.

Lucky popsicle, he thought, unable to tear his eyes away from the intensely erotic spectacle. He felt himself harden as heat rose to his face, and he applied himself to fervent sucking. He hoped to distract himself from Sebastian and his enticing display.

"So good," he groaned. "Raspberry with something spicy, right?"

"Mmm." Sebastian almost moaned. "Chipotle."

"Ahh." The sight and the sound of Sebastian's effort trumped the refreshing coolness of the frozen treat in Jesse's hand, over-shadowing the details of its exotic ingredients. All he could think of was Sebastian's mouth, and the way his lips wrapped around the cylindrical shaft. He wanted to feel that wet, incredible softness on the raging hard-on that was currently straining against the soft material of his pajama bottoms.

He yearned to reciprocate.

Jesse sucked again, working his tongue against the softening surface. Sebastian's hard cock wouldn't soften under his tongue. It would strain against his lips, smooth on the outside and steel-hard and delicious. He wanted to sample that taste, that texture. Skin as soft as that of Sebastian's cheek – probably even softer – sliding in and out of his mouth, pressing against his tongue.

Gah.

Jesse groaned out loud, hoping all of this would be over soon and Sebastian would never know. Instead, Jesse reviewed what he knew of the last three days.

He still didn't remember anything.

His fever had been alarmingly high.

Sebastian had been with him, taking care of him. He had stuck with him until his quarantine period was over.

He had been bathed, his clothing and sheets changed.

He had been, presumably, given enough liquids.

Sebastian, then, must have seen him naked.

The thought made heat rise up his neck again. Why did that matter? They had used the communal showers together on numerous occasions, they had both been naked then, and they had both ignored it. So why was it such a big deal now? There was a piece of information there somewhere, a little tidbit from several days ago that Jesse was searching for while sweet, slightly spicy raspberry juice made its way down his throat.

The fuzzy warmth of preheated seats.

The womb-like comfort of Sebastian's car.

"...then we broke up."

Tyler?!

That's what it was. Jesse began to piece together the whole scenario as information began to organize itself in his mind.

Sebastian and Tyler used to live together. They used to be a couple – and then they had broken up.

That meant... that meant Sebastian was gay?

Jesse sucked harder as his nervous habit took over. In times of stress, Jesse liked to have something, anything, in his mouth.

Then there was a vague recollection of some sort of a "boyfriend" comment. Connected to a sore fist. Jesse's half-willing mind recalled Tyler's gravelly voice, calling him Sebastian's 'boyfriend' after... oh God.

Oh, fuck.

"DID I REALLY punch my boss?"

Jesse's voice quivered a bit as he said that, and Sebastian suppressed a naughty grin. The very memory of Jesse's fist on Tyler's lantern jaw filled him with warm fuzzies.

"You did punch Tyler, yes." His matter-of-fact voice betrayed none of his excitement at the recollection.

Jesse pulled the red treat out of his mouth. What used to be a cylinder of raspberry puree, water, and electrolytes was now grainy, almost soft pointy stick. He gave it a good suck – it broke off in his mouth – and once he was done furiously sucking and swallowing, he licked his red-stained lips and looked at the ancient carpet. "Shit," he said. "I better start looking for a new job."

The thought overwhelmed the preceding insinuation that Jesse was Sebastian's boyfriend. He looked up, letting his head loll against the back of the sofa. Suddenly, he felt a fine shiver run through him, then another.

Job hunting.

"Are you feeling well, Jesse?" Sebastian's voice came to him as though from afar. He felt a hand touch his forehead and tried to reply but found that the shivers took over and he couldn't speak without an embarrassing clicking of his teeth.

"You're heating up again. Let's get you back to bed," he said. "Here, take these first."

Jesse swallowed the two pills Sebastian popped in his mouth, reveling in the soft caress of Sebastian's palm against his lips so much he didn't even think to ask what they were. He sipped some of the tangy lemonade from the workout bottle Sebastian handed him.

He didn't know how Sebastian found his workout bottle. At the moment, he was just grateful he didn't have to risk chipping his chattering teeth against a glass.

He felt Sebastian pull him up from the sofa and wedge his thinner shoulder under Jesse's arm, offering support.

Is that how he got me in and out of bed? In and out of the bath?

Next he felt soft pillows elevating his head, then friendly, soft hands tucked him under the sheet and pulled a warm, winter comforter under his chin.

"Ddd...don't ggg...go." He was barely able to speak, and it frightened him.

"You always say that," Sebastian said, allowing a small smile to lift the corners of his mouth.

"I...ddd...do?" Jesse exhaled.

"Yes. You do. Then I lie down next to you and you fall asleep."

The mattress dipped under Sebastian's weight. Jesse wiggled to make room as though it was second nature to him, and sighed as the weight of Sebastian's arm settled across his chest. When the slighter, warm body pressed through the comforter against him, Jesse felt himself relax at the sensation of heat and weight even as he shivered. He turned his head. Their eyes were so close together his vision blurred and he couldn't quite make out the details of

Sebastian's face.

"T...ttt...thanks."

He felt his eyes begin to tear up. Somebody had stayed with him, had taken care of him. He was so... so base, so unworthy of such attention. He was supposed to tough it out on his own, and now Sebastian got pulled from his daily duties. His workouts. His family.

The night Caleb had disappeared – they were barely seventeen at the time – Sebastian had decided not to ever depend on anyone again. His relationships followed a heart-wrenching pattern.

Jesse would get attached.

The loved one would die, or go into rehab, or get deployed and never return. Or mainline some bad stuff and disappear two days later.

Then Jesse would be alone again.

And Sebastian – he was kind, sweet, sexy, maybe even interested. He stayed and helped, and try as he might, Jesse felt that hopeful, fluttery warmth in his chest. The warmth of not being alone anymore, the hope of sharing his life with a friend. Or boyfriend.

Except Sebastian was used to better than Jesse. He had dated Tyler. Jesse knew, in the depth of his heart, that if he allowed the situation to turn into something serious, he was headed for a heartbreak of a lifetime.

He suppressed a ragged sigh and rolled his head away, not wanting Sebastian to know.

"AND I HAVE already expressed myself."

The words filtered to Jesse's ears through the cracked-open bedroom door and he felt the weight of resolve behind them. He stiffened with shock. Why would the quiet, mild-mannered Sebastian take such a tone of voice? The thought of something having gone wrong disturbed him. He slowly sat up and swung his legs to the floor, sinking his feet into his sheepskin slippers.

"Your argument is rife with flaws. Our market share has been diminishing due to our failure to adapt to changing consumer preferences. Our last line of special editions were nothing but the same, high-fat ice cream loaded with common candy and sundae sauces."

"…No.

"…Absolutely not."

"…Have you even looked at my ideas?…?…? No? … Hmm… I suggest that you do. If you truly wish to advance in this company someday, Mr. Warren, you'll find you need to listen less to our family of shareholders and more to your own gut feeling. Your opinions bear the imprint of my sister's stiletto heel."

JESSE SAT on the edge of his bed, the comforter draped over his shoulders and ears straining to hear the conversation going on in the other room.

Sebastian was working. Presumably, Sebastian was trying to turn the living room into his field office and telecommute as best as he could, running the New Products Division of Gillen Frozen Desserts, Inc., purveyor of gourmet ice cream, without spreading Jesse's germs around. He was fairly up to date on the source of Sebastian's frustration, and overhearing a snippet of his conversation with Renata's current fiancé did not surprise him whatsoever. The measured, icy tone, however… that rocked him back and made him pay attention.

He stood and shuffled to the bathroom. His body ached more today, even though his fever had taken another vacation. Jesse locked the door and turned the shower on. It was time to freshen up and rejoin the world of the living.

"MARKET RESEARCH shows the following trends…" Sebastian hummed under his breath, sitting ramrod straight on one of Jesse's wooden dinette chairs. His laptop was before him, a legal pad with hand-written notes was positioned by his left side. His work would move a lot faster if he were able to print out his research data instead of having to move from window to window. No matter – his predecessors had accomplished great deeds with naught but pen and parchment. It would reflect poorly to complain about his working conditions.

He bit his lip. Time came to be honest with himself. Sebastian had accomplished more while quarantined with Jesse than he would have ever had while butting heads with people at headquarters. They were either hidebound and territorial, or ambitious and aggressive. Either approach required careful management, and that took time.

Time which he'd rather spend on analyzing financial scenarios, formulating strategies, and implementing trial balloons.

His acute hearing picked up the sound of a shower being turned on, and the corners of his mouth lifted the slightest bit.

Jesse's feeling a lot better.

The shower stopped after a time, and Sebastian abandoned the image of a wet, naked Jesse in the shower with his hair all loose and snaking over his bronze shoulders and returned to market trends and today's lunch options.

He peered at the graph pulled off a website. The PDF file didn't blow up right and was too small to see.

New laptops and updated software always took him a while to learn, yet he seldom had the time to sit around and fiddle with menus and apps some idiot decided to move for the sake of novelty.

Had he been at his office, Paulette would have presented the data to him in a legible format. Had he been at his office alone, he'd have printed out the offending market trend, inflating the size of the graph using a paper copier. Now he could barely make out the words labeling the axes. He pushed his glasses up, letting his index finger slide up his nose, and frowned.

JESSE PULLED on a pair of jeans and, finding them a bit loose, he searched through his closet until he located an almost identical pair two sizes smaller. The old ones he'd had to buy once he had started gaining weight a couple of years ago. He used to hate them – he'd hated all they stood for – but over time, his 'fat jeans' became his 'skinny jeans'.

Dammit. Still too tight.

He squeezed his thighs in, and his butt, and worked hard to close the front to put the metal button through the hole.

So close.

Just half an inch more!

Jesse examined the problem. His flesh was compressible enough, but he needed extra leverage. Yeah, that was it. He lay down on the ground and pulled the sides up as far as they went, grasped the zipper pull, and gave an experimental tug.

Another, harder one.

And again.

His 'formerly fat, now skinny' jeans were now zipped half-way up and he could feel how close he was to putting those damn things on. Yet, whenever he pulled harder, the zipper pull slipped from between his fingers.

Fuckin' Tyler...

The thought of his boss' skinny butt arose in his mind and he felt envy – envy, and pain, and the fear of failure because, as he now saw with painful clarity, Tyler was an exemplary specimen of manhood and he had probably never even owned a pair of fat jeans. And now, knowing that Tyler used to know Sebastian rather intimately, and knowing that even the great and amazing Tyler got dumped, Jesse felt he had to exceed Tyler to win the chance to even look at Sebastian 'that way' again.

Tyler had a way of approaching problems which was none too subtle, and it occurred to Jesse that he, too, could resort to foul play.

Or force.

Jesse needed more force.

He got up from the floor and searched in the drawer of his nightstand, finally straightening with a victorious expression on his oval face and with a Leatherman Multitool in his hand. He flipped the device open, bypassing the knives and screws to open the pliers.

Lowering himself to the floor once again, Jesse grasped the zipper pull in his pliers, brought the two sides as close together as his other hand allowed, and he pulled… and pulled… then he exhaled and hollowed out his stomach and pulled again, and – voilà! The zipper was now closed all the way up.

With great care, not wanting to undo his hard effort, Jesse managed to close the button. Then he folded the Leatherman and, with awkward clumsiness caused by his extra-tight jeans, he stood up.

He looked in the mirror.

His legs looked thinner, his butt looked smaller, and his belly pudged over only a little bit.

But dammit, those love-handles. They muffin-topped over the back and sides of his jeans, making him look even fatter than before. With a resigned sigh he released the button, allowing the zipper to shoot open. He wiggled out of the too-tight pants and slipped into the too-loose ones, threw on a red and orange striped long-sleeve shirt, and padded out of his bedroom.

He stopped in the doorway. The sight before him stole his breath away. A gorgeous, golden-haired man sat at his dinette table. He was facing him but not seeing him. His fathomless, gray eyes were accentuated by the glasses he wore – the very glasses that were threatening to slide down the bridge of his nose. Sebastian's slender middle finger slid up his nose, pushing the black frames back where they belonged. The unconscious gesture drew a grin to Jesse's face.

That man looks so hot in those glasses!

The thought was as unbidden as it was unwelcome. Jesse's humiliation over a pair of jeans was quite enough and it would do him no good to fantasize.

But Sebastian did look damn hot in glasses. The frames were wide and angular, and the way Sebastian swept his hair up and over his ears created waves that invited Jesse's fingers to slide in and tug. He looked so serious just now, wearing his white work shirt even here, peering at something troublesome on his laptop. Jesse grasped the doorjamb tight, fighting the urge to go and take those glasses off Sebastian's nose and kiss that little frown between his eyes good-bye.

JUST AS Sebastian almost made out the letters on the stupid little graph on the screen of his laptop, his concentration was shattered by a soft gasp. Irritated beyond reason by his lack of a printer and a copy machine, he lifted his head up, only to see Jesse hanging onto the doorframe. He looked as though he'd gone three rounds sparring with Tyler, and it had taken all of Jesse's energy for the moment. He was up and showered and dressed, though, and moving under his own power. Sebastian counted that as a definite win. He nodded to him in greeting. "Did you sleep well?"

JESSE REMAINED silent, not trusting his voice. He watched Sebastian rise, his gorgeous, mercurial eyes focused on him with that adorable little frown right between them. He reached up to take his glasses away.

"No!"

Sebastian froze. "What?"

Jesse flushed. "I mean... I just didn't know you wore glasses." The sentence was lame and shed no light whatsoever on anything, but at least it was factually correct.

"Awful, aren't they?" Sebastian sighed. "Too bad I need them, but it's only for reading and computer work..."

"No!"

"No?" Sebastian intoned again, sounding intrigued.

"No, they're not awful. You look... good in them." Ravishing, hot, sexy, amazing, enticing, mysterious, strong, smart, kissable – Jesse didn't dare utter any of those words. Had he, perhaps, summoned the courage to say at least one, the glasses might have stayed perched on Sebastian's straight, aquiline nose but with the way things stood now, Sebastian removed them.

"You would not, perchance, have a working printer?" His voice was brimming with peevish irritation.

"Yeah, I have a printer – it's on the shelf by the sofa."

Sebastian's disposition brightened. "And would you, by any chance, have a copier?"

Jesse shrugged. "The printer copies and scans, if that's what you need."

"No… no, Jesse, I need a copier that will increase the size of the image for me."

Now that was different…

"What do you need to do?"

"This graph. It's so small. I can't read the thing."

"So…" Jesse took a deep breath, mindful of not cracking an amused grin. "So you want to print it out and enlarge it?"

"Exactly." Sebastian's expression was bordering on crestfallen.

"Why don't you just blow it up?" Jesse asked, studying Sebastian's face with the eye of an expert. He saw the eyebrows rise the slightest bit and the eyes widen. The angular features of Sebastian's lovely face were a study in control as he fought not to clench his teeth.

He doesn't know how.

"The software was upgraded last week." Frustration oozed from Sebastian's every pore.

"D'you mind if I give it a try?" Jesse asked, his tone neutral. He was, after all, accustomed to handholding both his colleagues and their clients through what he considered to be elementary computer processes.

Sebastian rose from his chair and nodded. Jesse took his place, clicked a few buttons, and the graph appeared in a new window, large and fully legible.

"Oh…" A small gasp, escaping Sebastian's lips, was his only reward.

Jesse grinned.

His stomach growled just then. With a look of relief, Sebastian shut his laptop and rubbed his eyes. "This is driving me nuts," he said with a sigh. "I need a bigger screen. And new glasses."

"Umm... " Jesse was about to mention he had an unused screen in the back of his closet, but Sebastian shook his head.

"Enough," he said. "How about some food?"

That's when Jesse realized he was finally feeling hungry again. Ravenous – but not for just anything. "Yeah," he said with a thoughtful nod. "Maybe."

"I'd like you to try something new," Sebastian said. "It's called pho."

SINCE THE little dining room table was cluttered with Sebastian's work, Jesse cleared off the few things that took up roost on the coffee table while Sebastian began to place small bowls of ingredients onto the scarred wood surface. The sofa was the only place to sit, but Jesse didn't at all mind sitting right next to Sebastian. Despite knowing better and trying hard not to act like a fool, his subconscious betrayed him every single time. Like now, when he positioned himself so they were brought closer together.

Heartbreak, here I come.

Sebastian took a pot off the stove and placed it on a folded kitchen towel in front of Jesse.

"So what is this?" The aromatics tickled Jesse's nose. He crinkled it and inhaled sharply while looking around for a box of tissues.

"If I was on a cooking show," Sebastian said with a wry smile, "I'd say this is a fragrant broth scenting the air with ginger, star anise and lemongrass, along with the pungent bite of fish sauce that whispers of salty seas and gives a good umami base."

Jesse rolled his eyes. "English, please!"

"Pho." Sebastian's face was dead-pan serious.

Jesse snorted. "That's not English!"

"It's Vietnamese." Sebastian thawed into hesitant half-grin. "It's a get-well soup."

"Oh, okay." Jesse leaned forward to examine the few bowls and glasses and their ingredients. "So what am I looking at, and what do I do with it?"

Sebastian pointed to a plate of finely minced greens. "These are basil, cilantro and mint. You put that in your bowl first. Then you put in a few slices of the hot peppers." He demonstrated, sprinkling a teaspoon of bright green, thin pepper slices in the bottom of his bowl.

Jesse mimicked him, being rather conservative with the peppers.

"Then you add some rice noodles… tofu and shrimp… shredded vegetables…"

Jesse added sliced red peppers and bean sprouts. His lunch looked like a colorful salad.

"Then you pour some of this hot broth over it, squeeze a bit of lime onto it, and eat it!"

It was the broth redolent of warming spices, which had scented the small apartment with the flavor of far-away places. Its heat warmed the protein and noodles, softened the vegetables, distributing the flavor of herbs and fresh pepper heat throughout. Jesse took another cautious spoonful. Sebastian watched him with amused interest.

"It's like a drowned salad," he finally declared.

"Hmm."

They ate in silence. Minutes passed.

"Is there more?" Jesse asked after a brief hesitation.

"You like it!" Sebastian smiled. It was the first genuine, for-real, no-holds-barred smile Jesse had seen him produce since the bike-giving episode with Tyler. He nodded, feeling stupid. Nobody's smile should have such power over him, and yet…

"It's real good. Really hits the spot, y'know?" His sinuses began to loosen, his nose started to drip, and Jesse turned to reach for his half-empty tissue box. He blew his nose. "Sorry."

"It's supposed to do that. It's an Asian equivalent of chicken soup."

"Heh – maybe only when you make it!"

Their eyes met. Their movements stilled, spoon arrested in

midair. A bean sprout dangled off the edge off Jesse's, threatening to fall.

The moment dragged on past the point of decency.

"Seb…"

"Jess…"

They both spoke simultaneously and stopped. In the past they would have laughed.

Not today.

"I'm not good enough," Jesse blurted out, beating Sebastian to the punch. Sebastian lifted a spoon of plain broth to his lips and sipped, savoring the flavor.

"Nonsense. You're more than 'good enough'. You are…" Sebastian let his eyes drop, suddenly focused on his soup. "You are kind. I… I appreciate that."

Jesse's eyes widened. "Me, kind? Bullshit! You're a lot nicer than I am. You've… you've been stuck here with me, taking care of me even though you could have gone home. You've cooked for me, you…"

Jesse couldn't say how much he appreciated Sebastian holding him when he'd felt at his lowest. Revealing something so personal would open him to rejection, and he didn't feel brave enough to face the almost certain possibility of that.

SEBASTIAN cleared his throat. "I merely tried to say that I appreciate the fact that you didn't make fun of me for my lack of computer skills. We bought new software packages, and I haven't had the time, or the motivation, truly, to spend the hours necessary on the introductory tutorial."

"You'd rather be swimming."

Sebastian matched Jesse's lopsided grin with a raised eyebrow, glad to see him doing better. "I'd rather… work on other things."

"What were you working on, anyway?" Jesse's question was meant to be innocuous, but it seemed to push a secretive button in his companion, whose expression grew impassive.

"Nothing of great importance."

"Okay," Jesse said, letting the subject drop. He rose, wanting to clear the dishes, when a bolt of pain shot up his back.

"Fuck." The expletive was followed by an immediate, "Sorry..."

Sebastian got up and circled around Jesse, examining his strained posture. "You're in pain."

"No shit, Sherlock."

"Jesse..." Sebastian stroked Jesse's wide shoulders with smooth hands, pressing hard on the muscles between the shoulder point and the neck. "Body aches and pains are a common symptom. I could help... if you let me."

"You could?" Jesse's voice came out a painful rasp.

"Yes. Lie down on the floor."

Sebastian shook out the sleeping bag he had been using and spread it on a clear patch of Jesse's carpeted floor. He watched him hesitate, and with great patience he said nothing. Satisfaction warmed his eyes as Jesse lowered himself to the ground, stretching his long body face down.

"Oh... and Jesse? Take your shirt off."

CHAPTER 10

JESSE FELT like he was a hundred-and-twenty, and hung over to boot. He lowered himself down to Sebastian's sleeping bag as though in slow motion, knowing that any sudden movement might exacerbate the shooting pain in his back. He didn't know what Sebastian had in mind, but remembered the stretching routine he learned from him at the pool, and how it had really helped with Jesse's soreness. Maybe there was a stretch he didn't know.

He settled down and turned his head to the side. Only Sebastian's feet –unsurprisingly graceful, clad in their black socks – were in his field of vision. The sleeping bag felt good beneath him though, cushiony, and he began to settle.

His weight sank into the soft, padded fabric. Lowering his guard, he began to relax even though he had no idea what to expect. After a moment or two he heard Sebastian's soft baritone again.

Except Sebastian had just asked him to take his shirt off.

Jesse didn't even bother trying to suppress his groan.

"Jesse."

"No."

With a sigh, a pair of knees settled on his blind side and warm, strong hands ran up and down his back.

"Such a lovely shirt, Jesse. It would be a shame if I stained it with massage oil."

Jesse buried his face into the padding under his nose. He felt treacherous heat spill up his skin, revealing his embarrassment.

And he was embarrassed.

He didn't want to be seen without his shirt. Not by Sebastian, whose physical form was so beautiful, whose, whose body was so well-proportioned and perfected by years of strenuous effort. His mind flashed to the vision of his workout partner, his sleek body cutting his way through water with efficient ease, its power restrained, long muscles in his strong back rippling as his legs executed that fluttery, almost imperceivable kick.

Now Sebastian, whose body was a controlled symphony in motion, would see his inadequate, abundant flesh spill all over his old, worn sleeping bag. The same Sebastian who had experienced the vastly superior physique of Tyler Easton, with whom Jesse could not even begin to compare.

Being shirtless at the pool was different, with both of them focused on counting laps, or fixing this or that technical issue. Here, now, being offered to Sebastian's gaze in all his imperfection, Jesse burned with acute embarrassment, as though every single one of his insecurities poured into the present moment.

"I'll… I'll keep it on for now. I think."

THE STONE-CUT, impassive set of Sebastian's face only served to conceal his frustration as his hands worked through the beefy cotton shirt. He thought he had discovered the site of the muscle spasm and began to knead the area hard enough for the muscle to relax, but not hard enough to tighten in defense. Jesse breathed quietly under him, tense and awkward.

"Jesse…"

"Yes?" The response was sharp and immediate.

"I need you to relax. If this is going to work I need you to close your eyes and breathe deeply. Allow your shoulders to soften… I found the spot and I'll work around it for a bit before I press on it directly."

Sebastian's soothing words paused as the heels of his hands described short, circular patterns up and down Jesse's back. He felt him settle somewhat.

Finally. But he still couldn't feel much through his shirt…

OKAY. I can do his. It's just a backrub…aaaaah.

Jesse's eyes closed. He puffed a gentle exhale, focused on his breathing. The offending muscle was beginning to loosen its painful hold as Sebastian's hands worked their magic. Jesse had never been touched like this before. His conscious mind kept track of his breathing pattern, but in the back of his mind he kept evaluating the way the other man's hands felt on his back. And they felt damn good. He bit back a little moan of pleasure as Sebastian moved toward the center of the knot. The woven cotton grated against his skin, but it was a small price to pay.

Startled, is eyes popped open as he felt Sebastian's body shift around him.

"I am going to straddle you, Jesse. Let me know if this causes you any pain."

Sebastian's weight settled as he lowered himself onto his buttocks, toned thighs against his hips, muscular calves brushing his own legs.

"Any pain?" Sebastian's voice was smooth and level and sexy.

Jesse fought to find his breath. "N… no."

Deft hands moved his shirt up just enough to slip under, and the soft heat of Sebastian's palms spilled across the skin of his lower back.

"Ahh… HA!" The shock of the skin-on-skin sensation made him jolt, and his insistent erection grated against the layers of fabric under him.

"Shh… Don't move." A bare hand, fingers outstretched, slid up his spine and pushed him back down.

"Relax, Jesse."

He was trying to relax with all his might; so hard, in fact, that his breathing shortened to ragged pants as he experienced the unprecedented pleasure of another's hands study the musculature of his back, caress it, tease it back into obedience.

So good... don't stop. Don't ever stop.

"I want you to remove your shirt, Jesse."

Sebastian's voice was gentle and firm all at once, bringing Jesse out of his state of utter bliss. He forced his eyes open and reconsidered.

The room was reasonably dim. Besides, with Sebastian sitting on him, it was likely his hated 'love handles' wouldn't even show.

He'd risk it.

He wiggled his hands under, undid two buttons, and yanked his shirt over his head. A button snagged in his long plait. Moments of frustration followed as he yanked at it in an effort to untangled himself.

"Let me help."

He felt Sebastian move up, his weight now hovering above the small of his back.

"I'll have to unbraid your hair." Somehow, Sebastian didn't sound upset at the prospect. Soon Jesse felt his hair falling onto his shoulders, strand by strand until Sebastian disentangled the offending button. His hair was a mess now, spilling loose to cover his face.

He felt palms press against his shoulders, running their way up his neck and all the way to the base of his skull.

"You're so tight. Let's see what I can do about that."

Jesse felt a warm weight settle on his lower back once more – Sebastian's legs, his ass, his hands all in close contact with Jesse's skin.

"Does that hurt?"

"No..." He exhaled.

"Good," Sebastian purred, letting his warm, kneading hands roam, making it harder and harder for Jesse to retain his hard-won control. The control that he had learned on the streets and in foster homes. The control that had kept him from letting anyone else close. The utter silence he perfected while taking care of his physical needs.

Surprised at himself, he felt his body relax, yielding to the touch of this interesting, enticing man. He let his eyes drift shut as a little moan of pleasure escaped him.

If he managed not to move too much, the issue below his waist would remain undiscovered.

SEBASTIAN cherished the bronzed skin under him with gentle strokes and fond eyes. He took his time and offered all his strength and skill. After a time, the kneading of his palms gave way to soft, fingertip caresses.

He was no blushing virgin, and knew exactly how his touch would affect the man sprawled beneath him. He stroked up Jesse's rib and bit back a gasp of his own pleasure as Jesse's legs tightened under him in an effort to still his hips. Sebastian's own breathing quickened at the thought that his touch aroused, titillated, frustrated.

Jesse might have seemed to be extroverted, but Sebastian noticed that he wasn't used to interacting with other people all that much. He was an enigma with a complicated history, a man wounded within, and Sebastian harkened to him, feeling a kindred spirit. He let his gaze feast on the sight of black ink spilled over smooth skin. A totem of some kind, and a bird, and something else.

He traced the tattoo with his fingertips, following its lines, trying to garner its meaning. More lines, now obscured by a flood of jet-black hair, waited to be explored on the shoulder.

Sebastian straightened and quietly removed his own shirt before he leaned forward to let his hands knead and stroke the tight muscles of Jesse's shoulders. He dug in, smoothing his way, digging the heel of his palm into the large, solid muscles underneath.

Jesse was strong and well put together, and Sebastian appreciated that. The expanse of skin beckoned to him and he obeyed its siren call. He let his body sink lower and lower until his flat belly skim the broad back, skin brushing skin in an electrified contact. Experimentally, he allowed himself to relax, covering Jesse's back with his body as his fingers ran tight circles along Jesse's scalp.

An arch of Jesse's back and a quiet moan was his reward.

He was so close – he inhaled the warm air, savoring the scent of Jesse's skin, Jesse's hair. That neck... when they ran together the week before Jesse had fallen ill, it had been drenched in sweat that he had wanted to lick off right then and there, run his tongue all the way up the strong muscles.

And now that his mouth was two inches away, the join of Jesse's neck to his broad shoulders begged for his attention.

He'd risk it.

He let his nose nuzzle its way through the curtain of Jesse's hair.

His lips touched the heated, fragrant skin. It was soft and warm, inviting, and its owner lay panting under him.

He allowed his lips to part, sucking on that tender place in a daring experiment, pushing all boundaries.

"AAAH!" A gasp. Then another, as his tongue flicked out to taste the sinuous neck.

So beautiful. You are so... Jesse.

HIS LITTLE sounds of pleasure became impossible to suppress. Jesse was appalled to feel his hips tilt, only to grind into the soft surface beneath him. He was so hard he'd burst if he didn't stop this...this...

He bunched his shoulders and rocked to one side and then to the other, dislodging his careless rider. Resting on his side, he felt exposed in the nudity of his torso, thankful that he wore his too-loose jeans.

"S... Sebastian."

What the hell are you doing?

"Jesse..." Sebastian's formerly gray eyes were glazed over and darkened with unmistakable want. A bare arm extended toward him, idle fingers toying with the pattern on his tattooed arm. "You're intoxicating, Jesse." He saw the handsome, chiseled face near him, soft lips slightly parted. "I am going to kiss you now." The voice bore a hint of command, but there was a pause between the warning and the action itself.

But... I never let any of Kerrick's cronies lay a hand on me.

"I'm not like Caleb." The raspy voice came out of Jesse's throat, barely audible.

Sebastian's progress halted with only a hand span dividing their lips. He closed his eyes and inhaled a deep lungful of air, then let it out with a soft hiss.

"Caleb?"

"A friend," Jesse whispered. "Tough history, there. He just disappeared one day."

Sebastian's lips hovered a handspan from his own. "Tell me?"

"Not now." Jesse turned his head, and Sebastian leaned away to give him space. "He'd do... do all kinds of stuff." The words tore their way out from Jesse's throat, under pressure, yearning to erupt. He never told anyone about Caleb. Anyone at all, and he didn't understand why he now felt this urgent need to share. He bit his lip and huffed. "It wasn't just drugs, but... he slept with other guys, for food and money. For a fix. I never did any of that. Or with- " Jesse sucked in a gulp of air and steeled himself. "With anyone."

"Not anyone, ever?" Sebastian asked, his tone flat.

"It's not that I didn't want to," Jesse rasped. "Just – I never felt safe. Not with Caleb, even though he wanted to." Jesse collapsed on the sleeping bag. "The needles, the johns. Y'know?"

"I know." Sebastian's heart twisted upside down and sideways. Jesse had had feelings for his best friend, and safety had won back then.

"And on the road, or on the street, even if the guy was hot, well..." Jesse's voice trailed off as he fixed his gaze on his popcorn ceiling. "I didn't know any of 'em real well. It didn't feel right."

Sebastian bit his lip. He had seen the want in Jesse's eyes. There was no mistaking the heated gaze that had traveled down Sebastian's limbs, his neck, that had caressed him over the last several weeks. And yet, despite the attraction and Jesse's age, he was inexperienced. A virgin in almost every way.

Incredible.

He reached out and placed his hand onto Jesse's, rubbing his thumb over Jesse's, relieved that Jesse didn't pull back. "Do you feel you don't know me?"

"No. I know you." Jesse met his eyes again. "I mean, we've been swimming and biking. And had lunches out. And running."

"Good times," Sebastian whispered.

"Yeah, real good times." Jesse turned his hand, sliding his palm against Sebastian's. "I got sick and you stayed."

"Taylor insulted me and you punched him." Sebastian squeezed Jesse's hand. "You're my friend."

"Yeah." Jesse drew a sharp breath. "A friend." More than just a friend.

Awesome, exciting, thrilling, erotic, arousing, gentle, passionate, soft and warm, caring.

Those were the words he wanted to say and was unable to let out.

Sebastian regarded him. "I would never hurt you."

Jesse allowed a sigh to escape. The problem down under wasn't as urgent anymore and he should have felt good about that, except now he missed Sebastian's touch and didn't know how to let all that magic happen again. His mind raced as he scrambled to right their course.

"Does your back hurt, too? Maybe I could... you know... "

UNDERNEATH his calm façade, Sebastian was seething with rage.

At himself, at the man Kerrick in Jesse's past, and once again at his own imperfect memory. How could a man Jesse's age feel so adrift, so lost in the world, to never trust another man intimately?

He raged at himself, too. How could he have forgotten that part of Jesse's history? Not that his friend... there was that cherished designation again, a friend… not that he had ever said much, but Sebastian had pieced together an outline of his tale, making use of the few words the man had let slip past his lips and from what he had recalled Renata had said about him.

Then there were those telltale signs of a rough past. Actions borne of an expectation that, someday, Jesse will end up on the street again, and the circles of his defenses kept people he might lose on the outside.

He felt his anger soften into sympathy. Jesse was strong – so very strong inside and so determined – he had come so far already. He had graduated college after only having learned to read as a teenager. Sebastian loved the fire in those eyes, the way lightning flashed during a spirited discussion. The way they settled while Jesse was focused on a problem. Now they were a dull brown. Still tired from the flu, but also exhausted from letting Sebastian push him past his comfort zone.

"I am sorry, Jesse."

"What for?"

"I didn't mean to push."

"So why did you do it? Kiss my neck like that?" A bit of fire kindled in his eyes again, making Jesse's expression wild and feral.

Truth was the best policy with a wild thing.

"I've wanted to do that for weeks now."

"For weeks? You're lying."

A bit of hurt resonated in Sebastian voice, as he asked, "What makes you think I'd lie?"

"'Cause… 'cause I was, like, even bigger then. No way could you feel attracted to me like that."

"Do you think so little of me? Do you think I'm that shallow?" Sebastian sat up, filtering most of his hurt out of his voice.

"I'd never think that! You're… you're amazing. I can't understand why a guy who used to be with someone like Tyler would be interested in a nobody like me!"

Ah.

JESSE SAW the thinly veiled hurt. He felt bad about it, but

there wasn't much he could do. The man had kissed him. On the neck. He had felt Sebastian's hard length press into his back as he had done so and it had made him stir and grind into the sleeping bag – he had almost lost it.

Then again, he had said he had wanted to do that for weeks. Sebastian Gillen was an adult. He was staying in Jesse's apartment voluntarily and had been so kind. The memory of his warm body in the middle of the night made Jesse stir with comfortable heat.

Jesse reached out, tentative and slow, toward Sebastian's bare shoulder. Sebastian had that face on again, the one where Jesse just knew he was seething underneath but showed nothing to the outside world. He let his rough fingertips brush Sebastian's skin.

Their eyes met.

"Don't be mad."

"Not mad at you." Sebastian's growl turned breathy under Jesse's fingertips.

"I'm sorry. I'm really sorry." Jesse's words spilled out like a waterfall. "I've never kissed a guy before. I do… I lack experience in a lot of this stuff, y'know."

His keen eyes observed Sebastian's expressionless face. He was like a statue, motionless and pale.

"You said you won't hurt me," Jesse continued as he propped himself up to his elbow so he could study Sebastian's face. He searched for the right words. "I… I trust you, Sebastian."

He looked up into those gray, stormy eyes. The color wasn't so cold anymore as sparks flew behind those billowing clouds. Jesse leaned closer, drawn by their depth, and didn't flinch when he felt Sebastian's hand slide up his arm and behind his neck.

A peevish expression ghosted over his face, dissipating as Sebastian relaxed.

"I know how you hate to repeat yourself," Jesse whispered.

"Yeah," Sebastian exhaled, the colloquial word transforming him into a different man.

"You're gonna kiss me now."

"Yes."

Their lips came closer, Jesse's neck pulled forward, their eyes not quite locked.

Soft. Sebastian's lips were so soft. Yet powerful, too.

Jesse let him lead – his experience was limited to the few kisses Renata had allowed– and was surprised to feel the other man's tongue skim across his lower lip. His whole body jolted at the sensation that settled in the base of his balls.

'Good' didn't begin to describe how incredible it felt.

Then that tongue invaded Jesse's mouth, gently exploring, pausing so they both could breathe.

Jesse was aware of every inch separating their bodies. Brushes of skin were bright shocks of sensation. His eyes threatened to close again as he whimpered a needy moan. With the slightest nudge, Sebastian made him fall back onto his back. His hand slid down Jesse's chest, teasing his nipple along the way but he didn't feel anything. All of his sensation was pooled to one place only.

"Careful…" Jesse gasped in warning.

"I know. It's supposed to be like this." The reassuring voice was accompanied by the slender hand slipping under the loose waist-band of his jeans, cupping the erect length, pink tip peeking from underneath his briefs.

He bucked his hips with a gasp. "Sebastian!"

Few more strokes. His jeans were undone and pushed off his hips.

He forgot to think about the way he looked, about the way he sounded. His whole world consisted only of that pleasurable sensation, the feeling of somebody else touching him the way he often touched himself. Yet Sebastian's hand felt so much better than his own and he didn't know why, nor did he have the wherewithal to question the fact at the time.

Soft fingers slipped his briefs off. Jesse gasped at the shock of cooler air against his heated skin. The cool shock didn't last long. The wet warmth of Sebastian's mouth followed.

He whimpered and bucked his hips up twice and threw his arm across his face, biting it hard to muffle the feral shout that accompanied the cresting wave of unbearable pleasure.

SEBASTIAN gave a satisfied hum as he inhaled the spicy, musky smell of Jesse's groin. He slid his lips over the still-hard length, swallowing the pungent load. He glanced up. If this was Jesse's first time, no wonder he went off like a roman candle!

Jesse's eyelids slitted open as Jesse peeked down at him in curious exploration. Sebastian saw shock in those enticing eyes – and something else as well – as he dragged his tongue from base to tip and licked the extra come off his lips.

He let Jesse pull him up and into a close hug. His large hands were warm and reassuring.

"I… I don't know what to say."

"Did you like it?" Sebastian inquired with a gleam of mischief in his eyes.

"Fuck.... I never knew it could feel like that. That was just fucking amazing." He nuzzled his face into Sebastian's curls, inhaling his scent. It was light, clean like the warm summer rain, and just as comforting. Jesse slipped his hand around Sebastian's waist, pulling him closer.

THE HARD and promising shape of Sebastian's hard cock pressed his thigh through two layers of fabric. He felt Sebastian rub into him, and when he lifted his head, he found Sebastian was biting his lower lip with an expression of intense concentration.

I've gotta do something about that.

But what, dammit?

Trying to imitate Sebastian's actions, he slid his hand down to cup the hard, straining rod in his pants. He schooled his expression into a serious, stoic mask. Imitating Sebastian without cracking up was harder than he would've guessed.

"Sebastian… take your pants off."

THE LAST thing Sebastian expected was reciprocity. Jesse was, after all, new at this. Jesse also had his pride, however, and wasn't the kind of a man who would leave a debt unpaid. Yet the seriousness of Jesse's command amused him. He was obviously learning by example, following Sebastian's lead.

He unfastened his own trousers and slipped them off, tossing them over the arm of the sofa above them. Only his briefs were left.

"You don't have to, Jesse."

"Oh, but I want to. I want to make you feel as good as you made me feel." Jesse's hand meandered down Sebastian's chest, making a brief stop at the nipple, tweaking it gently.

"Feels good…" Sebastian exhaled, encouraging.

"Yeah… you're so smooth…" Jesse's fingertip ran over his incredible skin with a gentle caress, enjoying the contrast of the soft and hard, with toned muscles playing underneath. He propped himself up on an elbow, and as he leaned over him, Jesse's curtain of hair tickled his neck.

He dipped his head, letting their lips come into shy, hesitant contact. Sebastian carded his fingers through the black, silken strands. He felt small in Jesse's shadow. Delicate, with fine-boned hands compared to Jesse's warm paws.

However did the man buy gloves?

Jesse was strong and broad, and Sebastian reveled in it. He basked in the feeling of being protected and explored, secure in the knowledge that Jesse, despite his inexperience, would handle him with gentle care.

JESSE LET his weight rest on the man beneath him halfway, the awareness of his extra weight always in the back of his mind.

"Jess…"

"Yeah?" Jesse whispered as he kissed the corner of the lips.

"I won't break," Sebastian whispered. "I love to feel you on top of me."

"Yeah?" Jesse adjusted his position, exerting more pressure, pressing Sebastian into the sleeping bags. "This okay? I'm heavy."

"Not so heavy." Sebastian wiggled under him. "Just secure."

Jesse's cock began to harden again. All that skin, the scent – the kisses. He wondered if he could live off the kisses alone. He rutted against Sebastian, elbows anchored by his shoulders, lips brushing in disrupted attempts at yet another delicious and arousing kiss.

"Ahh… feels so good." The hands in his hair tightened and Jesse felt heat shoot to his groin once again. He pressed against the hollow of Sebastian's hip, feeling his underwear. The suddenly too-coarse fabric had to go. He hooked his thumb under the elastic and tugged it off.

Sebastian lifted his slender hips, aiding his effort. The offending piece of white cotton was gone, and now he rubbed against the smooth ivory skin. A deep rumble emanated from his chest as Jesse realized he could easily come again.

JESSE GASPED, responding to Sebastian's touch as sharp nails and hot fingers drew fire trails down his sides, his back. Sebastian wiggled under Jesse's welcome weight, drawing lines down hips that were now centered directly over Sebastian's.

Jesse was now over him, settled between Sebastian's vulnerably splayed knees. Jesse lifted his hips free and thrust low, gently exploring the softness of Sebastian's sac, the smooth globes of his ass that were pressed into a half-open crack.

Experimentally, Jesse pushed the head of his cock down there, past where he could see. A sharp intake of breath, wild eyes, a whimper that escaped Sebastian's red, swollen lips.

"Do we have condoms?" Sebastian gasped.

"No." Jesse stilled, then thrust his hips back and away. "I want you so bad," he whispered. "You can be my first everything."

"Baby steps." Sebastian redirected him until their hot lengths touched, smooth and hard.

They both gasped.

Jesse's arms just about collapsed, and he barely caught himself on his elbows, kissing Sebastian's closed eyelids, his forehead. Sebastian traced Jesse's jaw with his eager lips, aware of a hint of stubble and an earthy scent.

Sandalwood?

Sebastian inhaled the scent of the long, silken hair that fell around him like a waterfall. He jutted his hips up once again in search of that delicious contact, gripping Jesse's waist, pulling him down. His hands were full – soft flesh spread under his palms and fingers. He squeezed, unable to stop himself.

"Wait…" Jesse gasped, self-conscious of a part of his body that was less than shapely in his eyes. Their eyes met, and Sebastian understood.

"No," he said, shaking his head, suddenly understanding. He met Jesse's dark eyes. "This is part of you. All of it, and I'll have you as you are." His voice came out level and firm, the insistent tone being just shy of being a command.

I want you Jesse.

I love you Jesse.

Every bit of you, every inch, every smile, every stubborn ounce.

He let his hand slip off his hip and between them, grasping their aroused lengths together. A bit of lube would've helped – but he'd be better prepared the next time. For now, Sebastian was drowning in Jesse, in his taste and his smell, hiding beneath the waterfall of his incredible hair.

He stroked, Jesse gasped.

He squeezed, Jesse thrust.

He twisted, Jesse's mouth anchored itself at the join of neck and shoulder. The powerful suction and the barely restrained, painful bite made Sebastian lose control and he came, splattering them both with the hot, slick seed of his nearly-silent climax.

JESSE FELT Sebastian's cock twitch and pulse and he heard the sharp inhale and the low hiss of pleasure as the body beneath him shuddered, all conscious control shattered beyond recognition. The sight of the flushed, sweat-streaked face and the smell of his jizz tipped him over and he bit down harder in a vain effort to silence his shout.

Their flushed limbs were covered with a sheen of sweat as they rested, tangled together on a sleeping bag on Jesse's floor.

"Sorry," Jesse breathed, kissing the bite mark that glared, angry and red, from Sebastian's pristine skin. Breathing slowed and heart rates were approaching normal once more when Jesse's cell phone rang far away in the bedroom.

"They'll leave a message," Jesse said with a purr, pulling Sebastian's back against his chest.

A few moments later, Sebastian's cell phone went off in the pocket of his trousers somewhere above their heads.

"Maybe I should get that," Sebastian intoned.

Jesse pulled him even closer, licking the sweat off the elegant curve of his neck. "Maybe not."

"Jesse." The tone held a note of admonishment.

"Don't go. You have to stay and comfort me."

"Comfort you?" Sebastian pulled the edge of the sleeping bag over them, conserving what body heat remained, and turned in Jesse's arms to face him.

"Yeah. Y'see, I'm traumatized." Jesse's eyes grew serious and his voice held an uncertain quaver to it. Sebastian lifted the edge of his eyebrow in puzzlement, unsure whether or not Jesse was joking.

"Yeah. You may not realize it, but… you're my first lover, aside from my trusty right hand here, and I am not sure how to feel about that. So… just stay with me, okay?"

And despite the pleasure and the closeness, Jesse did in fact seem just a bit awkward, and uncertain, and his humorous bluster did little to cover the undercurrent of fear he was trying to disguise.

"I'll stay with you." Sebastian slid his arms around him, looking for a good position so he could stay that way without having to move. His shifting, however, made the drying fluid on their skin stick unpleasantly. "Although we should clean up."

He rose and made his way to the bathroom on unsteady feet, keenly aware of Jesse's gaze. It felt like a caress, like a seedling that could grow into a mighty tree, given a chance. His breath stuttered at the thought. It had been a while since he let anyone into his life. He was boring compared to Jesse's exotic appeal, timid next to the brash courage borne of Jesse's desperate history.

Yet Jesse wanted to be with him.

He came back with a towel. As he helped Jesse clean off, he avoided his eyes. This was serious, more so than he'd expected.

He was falling...

"Now what?" Sebastian whispered.

"What do you mean?"

Sebastian settled next to Jesse again. "I'm not exactly a great catch, so... do we have a plan?"

Jesse caressed him with a thoughtful gaze. Then he pulled him down, drawing him into a warm, cozy embrace.

"No need to overthink this, yeah? We get along. Let it play itself out, see what happens."

Sebastian twisted in his arms to meet Jesse's eyes. "Okay. We take a chance. We ride this wave and see where it takes us. But tomorrow?"

A lazy smile lit up Jesse's face. "One day at a time, right? Today, we rest. Tomorrow, we get up and train."

"For the triathlon?"

"Yeah, for the triathlon." Jesse's eyes were dark and warm, inviting him in. "We're already training partners, and we'll work on the boyfriend part one day at a time."

"Just like that," Sebastian said. The simplicity of Jesse's plan was new and refreshing. He had been looking for a fresh start for quite a while, and now, with Jesse, he could start his life all over again. Work, family, swimming, even picking up their bikes. All those unfinished parts of his life were going to get an overhaul while he ran with Jesse, fed him good food, and nurtured him with a galaxy of kisses.

The boyfriend part.

One day at a time.

THE END

Readers love Kate Pavelle:

Wild Horses
"...the unexpected twist ... the relationship between the men will never be the same... I loved this book!"   -   USA Today

"This book will pull you and make you love and feel for the characters."

-   World of Diversity Fiction Reviews

"Read this book. Even if horses do nothing for you, read this book for its show of healing powers. It made me feel so good."
-   My Fiction Nook

Zipper Fall
"Thank you, Kate Pavelle, for this remarkably romantic thriller, which revealed that self-reliant does not necessarily mean alone."
-   Rainbow Book Reviews

-

A murder mystery romance filled with suspense, adventure and obsessions.
-   Gay List Book Reviews

Broken Gait
"A surprising and unique story, _Broken Gait_ is an excellent read."
-   USA Today

Breakfall
"This was a stunning read and I must admit to losing a bit of sleep over this for the images were just so true and real."
-   Multitaskingmommas Book Reviews

"The ending has hope, sweetness, and the promise of another Sean and Asbjorn book that comes like a blow to the face. I can't wait."
-   Cryselle's Bookshelf

Swordfall

"... a thrilling adventure, full of excitement, hot sex, menace and ultimately a love between two men that won't be stopped short of death."

- USA Today

Landfall

"This is a great ending to the series and another book that demonstrates Ms Pavelle's broad knowledge of science and martial arts as well as her vivid imagination."

- Becky Condit

Relativistic Phenomena

"Relativistic Phenomena is a sweet novella, and the tentative relationship between Tony and Ken is quite endearing."

- Scuttlebutt Reviews

On the Run (a Cancelled Czech Files book)

"... a journey on the run from the secret police as they bravely immigrated to America... a book to read with your entire family."

- USA Today

More by Kate Pavelle:

<u>With Mugen Press</u> (www.mugenpress.com)

Relativistic Phenomena
Kickass Anthology
On the Run (Cancelled Czech Files book)

Coming soon:

Lucky Starflowers (Steel City Stories)
Waterkin (urban fantasy YA)

<u>With Dreamspinner Press</u> (www.dreamspinnerpress.com)

Wild Horses (Steel City Stories)
Zipper Fall (Steel City Stories)
Broken Gait (Steel City Stories)
Breakfall (Book 1 of Fall trilogy)
Swordfall (Book 2 of Fall trilogy)
Landfall (Book 3 of the Fall Trilogy

Coming soon:

Sire (Steel City Stories)

ABOUT THE AUTHOR

Kate Pavelle learned to use a gas mask in first grade. She fired her first AK47 in her sixth grade civil defense class. Her first dog was a wolf hybrid stolen from the Czechoslovak border guard. Her eccentric father blew out the windows of their house with a stun grenade - on purpose. Unlike his chemical explosions —those were always by accident. Her high-stakes, high-adrenaline childhood leaves her searching for the next exciting thing. Martial arts and travel and rock climbing. Horses and cookies and toxic mushrooms. Medieval combat and children and brain-tanning deer hide in her Pittsburgh driveway.

Her quest resonates through her mystery thrillers and romances, matched only by her drive to share the fun with her readers. Kate once knew the hunger of being a political refugee and the terror of being pursued by government agents. She imbues her characters with her own struggle for survival, excellence, and world domination. Only the dead bodies are imaginary.

FOLLOW KATE!
Facebook - Kate Pavelle
Twitter - @katepavelle
www.katepavelle.com
Or tune in for her Thursday Morning Coffee Blog on www.
katepavelle.wordpress.com.

www.ingramcontent.com/pod-product-compliance
Lightning Source LLC
Chambersburg PA
CBHW060429130626
46555CB00005B/2283